HAMISH
AND THE
BABY BOOM!

Look Out For

HAMISH
AND THE
WORLDSTOPPERS

HAMISH
AND THE
NEVERPEOPLE

HAMISH
AND THE
GRAVITYBURP

HAMISH
AND THE
BABY BOOM!

BY DANNY WALLACE

ILLUSTRATED BY
JAMIE LITTLER

SIMON & SCHUSTER

LONDON   NEW YORK   SYDNEY   TORONTO   NEW DELHI   STARKLEY

irst published in Great Britain in 2018 by Simon and Schuster UK Ltd
A CBS COMPANY

1 3 5 7 9 10 8 6 4 2

Simon & Schuster UK Ltd
1st Floor, 222 Gray's Inn Road
London
WC1X 8HB

www.simonandschuster.co.uk

Simon & Schuster Australia, Sydney
Simon & Schuster India, New Delhi

A CIP catalogue record for this book is available from the British Library.

PB ISBN 978-1-4711-6782-9
eBook ISBN 978-1-4711-6783-6

Printed and bound by CPI Group (UK) Ltd, Croydon, CR0 4YY
Simon & Schuster UK Ltd are committed to sourcing paper that is made
from wood grown in sustainable forests and supports the Forest Stewardship
Council, the leading international forest certification organisation. Our
books displaying the FSC logo are printed on FSC certified paper.

For Freddie Batie
(and his big sister Immy)
From your pals,
Danny & Jamie

Frinkley Starfish

More news than you get in Starkley!

FRINKLEY VOTED BEST PLACE TO LIVE NAMED FRINKLEY

For the ninetenth year in a row, Frinkley has been named the 'best place to live named Frinkley'!

'This is such an honour,' said the Mayor of Frinkley, Jikky Nibs, who came up with the award and was the only judge. 'It's such a surprise to be nominated and even better to win!'

Mayor Nibs was delighted Frinkley fought off stiff competition from the likes of Frinkley, Frinkley, Frynkeley and Frinkley, all of which are different Frinklies and therefore not as good as our Frinkley.

'Let's see if we can make it twenty wins in a row next year!' added Mayor Nibs, who then winked and said that as he gets the only vote he had a pretty good feeling about that.

CRIME UP AGAIN – WHO COULD IT BE?

For a third month in a row, crime is up in Frinkley, though no one knows exactly why. Mrs Jibberson found all her cat bowls had gone missing on Friday night. Who is doing this? One thing's for sure – it can't be someone from Frinkley…which just leaves everywhere else!

arkley Stinks!

Horatia Snipe

it just me or does Starkley ink? And I'll tell you what – 's the kids!

Everybody knows that children stink of spiders' legs and wet dog – but in Starkley they smell even worse!

Something about that town just doesn't sit right with me. What are they so proud of?

Why do they seem so... happy?

As far as I can see, all they've got is a sweet shop run by a mad old woman and a town clock that used to run fast, but now isn't even interesting enough to do that! If you ask me...

Continued on pages 2, 3, 4, 5, 6, 7, 8, 9 and 12.

Did You Know?
Five Fantastic Frinkley Facts!

1 Frinkley is an anagram of 'Awesome!' using different letters!
2 No one has ever fallen over in Frinkley!
3 It was Frinkley that first spotted the moon!
4 Frinkley is the most popular word in the English language!
5 Soup, peanuts and purple were all invented in Frinkley!

WARNING FROM THE AUTHOR:

The following opening chapter contains deeply disgusting details of a horrific nature.

If you are a sensitive child, prone to vomiting, please immediately fetch a bin.

If you don't have a bin, fetch a smaller child with large pockets.

If no smaller children are available, use a grown-up's shoes.

1
The Small
Wee hours

It was a minute after your bedtime, and in the small town of Frinkley Nurse Pickernose was checking on all the new babies at the hospital.

There were twenty-two of them in the nursery that evening, each one gently sleeping in his or her own little cot, and all lined up in a perfectly lovely circle.

There was tiny Ringo Togs.

And little Bottletop Baxter.

And cute, wee Orangina Sniffle.

This roomful of babies was a particularly good roomful of babies. Each one was incredibly sweet and well behaved.

'Aw,' smiled Nurse Pickernose to herself. 'Night-night, my Frinkley wrinklies.'

This was a woman who loved babies almost as much as she loved kebabs, and this was a woman who loved kebabs. She loved their little whimpers and their little sighs.

The sighs of the babies, I mean. Not the kebabs.

She loved their baby yawns too, and the way they'd do those very fast little baby bottom burps. 'Just some love escaping!' she'd joke.

Nurse Pickernose adored her job and she'd been at the hospital forever. She'd even been born there. Her whole life was at this place and there was nowhere she'd rather work. She would skate to Frinkley Hospital every day on her medical skateboard, thinking that this was a job she would cherish always.

Nurse Pickernose decided that she would let the babies sleep, but, just as she began to close the door to the nursery, she heard a very quiet noise.

FSSSSSSSSSSSSSSSSSSS.

Her eyes blinked in the darkness. She crumpled them up, as if that would help her see better.

The noise began to get louder.

FSSSSSSSSSSSSSSSSSS.

It sounded like someone had left a small garden hose on.

She blinked again, and stepped back into the room and turned on a light.

What she saw shocked her.

A little baby boy was lying on his back. Peeing.

But not just peeing.

Really peeing.

He was peeing so quickly and so powerfully that a jet of pure baby pee was shooting straight up into the air through his blanket and down onto the floor!

Nurse Pickernose just stood and stared for a second. She'd

never seen anything like it. It formed a perfect curve in the air and looked like some kind of weird liquid rainbow.

She sprang into action, grabbing a towel and pounding towards the baby to stop the fountain of pee.

'There!' she said, pressing the towel down with both hands, the way a plumber might quickly stop a leak. The baby smiled a satisfied smile, then opened its eyes and stared straight at Nurse Pickernose.

And, a second later, from right behind her . . .

FSSSSSSSSSSSSSSSSSSS.

Nurse Pickernose turned to see a *new* jet of wee shooting through the air, from a *totally different* baby!

Up, up in the air it went.

Down, down on the floor it spittered and spattered.

'No, Julio!' she said, sternly, and with wide eyes.

She lunged to cover the second baby's wet jet with a towel. But as she did so – oh, no! – something warm and wet struck her on the back of the head.

PEE!

She whirled round. The first baby was still going! And he was still staring straight at her . . .

Nurse Pickernose needed new towels and she needed them now!

She ran for the door but was stopped in her tracks. A third baby had started peeing right where she wanted to go and this little guy was a brute! The pee was raining down in front of her like he was using a Super Soaker!

The floor was really wet now and, as Nurse Pickernose tried to dodge and weave her way through the golden arches, she slipped head over heels onto the floor.

THWACK!

She slid about, her sensible shoes skidding around on the slick tiles, then looked up.

NO!

Four babies were peeing!

Five!

NOW SIX!

Short bursts of wee, starting and stopping, shooting through the air like some kind of fountain display you'd see in a fancy shopping centre.

First the ones on the left would shoot a burst!

Then the ones on the right!

THERE ARE BABIES PEEING EVERYWHERE!' she yelled, but there was no one there to listen. Her words hung in the air, getting **wetter** and **wetter** from the **plippering** and **sloppering** that now drowned them out.

She knew it was down to her to sort this mess out. So, with renewed determination and putting all her training to good use, Nurse Philately Pickernose ran and slid across the floor, grabbed three fresh towels and flapped them out, like a bullfighter with a cape.

She strode towards the centre of the circle of cots and, like lightning, covered one baby.

She quickly turned and flung a towel over another.

She whipped a new towel round and – **THWACK** – flicked it at a third baby.

It was working!

But more baby boys had started peeing now – she couldn't count how many – and now it was like they were AIMING FOR HER!

Fast, sharp jets of pee started randomly shooting out of all the baby boys, arcing through the air straight at Nurse Pickernose.

'**AAAARGH!**' she yelled, as the baby girls blew giant raspberries and flung great whips of drool from their cots.

What had she done to deserve this?

Every time she flapped out another towel to stop one jet, another would drench her from a different angle!

If she threw a towel at one baby, the baby behind her would shoot a burst!

If she threw a towel at a baby behind her, pee would whizz from a totally different one!

This was like **Whack-a-Mole . . .**

'**HELP!**' she shouted. '**SOMEONE HELP ME!**'

But no one could hear poor Nurse Pickernose as she ran out of towels and began to scream. She was alone. At the worst baby shower ever.

Then, as if someone had pressed an accelerator button, every single baby boy started peeing quicker and more powerfully in unpredictable bursts.

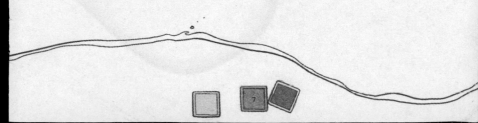

It was too much for Nurse Pickernose to deal with. All she could do was retreat to a cupboard, where she would spend the rest of the night, huddled in a corner, termbling.

And that was the night Nurse Philately Pickernose decided to retire.

If you've been affected by any of the issues raised in this chapter, best keep it to yourself, it's embarrassing.

Oh, Hi, Hamish!

Hamish Ellerby arrived at **FRINKLEY HOSPITAL** and immediately wanted to turn back again.

Hamish did *not* like hospitals. And he wasn't particularly keen on Frinkley. So I think you can guess what he thought about **FRINKLEY HOSPITAL**.

It was a large, long building painted perfectly white, apart from hundreds of little red crosses on every brick in the walls.

'We'll be straight in and out!' said Hamish's mum, and she was right, because she'd never been very good at revolving doors. Before they knew it, they were out on the street again.

When they finally made it inside, they stopped at the kiosk near the entrance and Mum started looking at the flowers.

They were here in Frinkley because Hamish's mum wanted to visit a lady called Mrs Quip. They'd become great friends recently. Mum said she liked Mrs Quip because she was someone who would listen to her complaining without . . . well . . . complaining. Mrs Ellerby worked at Starkley Council in the Complaints Department, you see, meaning she normally spent all day listening to other people complaining. Once, so many people complained that she actually filed a complaint herself about all the complaints she was getting. But she wouldn't need to do that again, because Mrs Quip loved listening to her.

Mrs Julie Quip worked in the Paper Cup Department, ordering paper cups for places that needed paper cups. As a result, anything that didn't involve paper cups was immediately very interesting to her, and Mum's work seemed oh-so glamorous and exciting in comparison.

The Quips lived just round the corner from the Ellerbys, on Diablo Close, and had recently welcomed into the world a bouncing baby boy called Boffo.

Starkley didn't have its own hospital any more so all new babies were born in Frinkley. Starkley just had a school nurse called Blind Mary, and she wasn't really someone you wanted to give you stitches and so on. But Hamish never felt very comfortable coming to Frinkley these days.

I don't know if you've ever noticed, but sometimes towns that are very close together don't seem to get on that well.

I mean, did you hear about Great Nordic and Peppermill?

They got on so badly one Christmas that they all turned their houses away from each other in a huff!

Or how about Thack and Lower Stumpy?

All the inhabitants of Thack had paid other people to vote for a very unusual mayor in Lower Stumpy. Which is why Lower Stumpy's new mayor was a very powerful earthworm named Bonbon.

I suppose these bickering towns are a bit like siblings. That's definitely what it felt like with Starkley and Frinkley.

And Frinkley was very much the flashier big sister. It had a **bowling alley** and a **Laser Quest arena** and you could buy hot dogs almost anywhere – even in the shoe shop. *And* there was a rumour they were getting a **popcorn fountain!** Also, unlike in Starkley, the funfair came to Frinkley *twice* a year. Once because it had to and a second time because it missed everyone so much.

The problem was, all these roller discos and rock concerts had gone to the their heads. They walked a bit differently in Frinkley. More confidently. Frinklings held their heads a little higher, which was why it was easier for them to look down on people.

It didn't used to be this way. Once, the two towns had got along perfectly well. But in the last few months in particular, it really seemed as if Frinkley had it in for Starkley.

'Right!' said Mum. 'These are the perfect flowers!'

It was a beautiful bouquet in the shape of a hot dog. Frinkley was so cool.

As Hamish and his mum walked through the foyer towards Mrs Quip's room, he couldn't help but notice that the hospital didn't seem quite as tidy as it should've been. A fire extinguisher had been knocked over. There were magazines all over the floor too.

And, as Mum forged onwards, Hamish was shocked when a man nearby suddenly screamed.

'Ow!' he shrieked. 'Who did that?!'

A few people turned round to see what all the fuss was about.

'Come on!' he shouted. 'Own up! Who just flicked my bottom?! Because someone just flicked me on the bottom!'

A few people shrugged and shook their heads, as if to say, 'It definitely wasn't me who flicked you on the bottom!'

But the man thought he knew exactly who'd flicked him on the bottom.

'I bet it was YOU!' he said, pointing at another man, and he moved a pram out of the way so he could stride over and tell him off.

'My wallet's gone!' shouted a different man. 'I had it right here!'

He was standing next to his wife, looking incredibly confused. He was wearing his infant son on his chest in one of those baby carriers, and frantically checking all his pockets.

'Thief! There's a thief in our midst!' cried his wife, as they turned round to check the floor.

A moment later . . .

BANG!

'Help!' yelled a lady in a tiny hat. 'I'm stuck in the revolving door!'

She began to THUMP, THUMP, THUMP on the glass.

How had she managed that? A few people dashed over to help, but soon found themselves slipping and sliding on nuts and bolts that had somehow come loose.

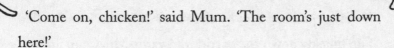

'Come on, chicken!' said Mum. 'The room's just down here!'

Hamish would normally have followed her straight away. But something made him turn and look back once more.

People were squabbling.

Checking their pockets.

Wagging angry fingers in each other's faces.

But if you ignored all of that and looked a little closer . . .

You could see babies smiling and smirking.

You could see a baby slapping the head of an old man, asleep in a chair, like it was a bongo.

But more importantly . . .

You could hear a tiny baby chuckling to himself in the pram next to the man with the flicked bottom . . .

You could see a little baby boy sucking on something square and leathery and wallet-like close to his dad's chest . . .

And you could see a tiny baby girl with short hair in stumpy pigtails sitting, giggling, on the floor by the revolving door. A giggle that stopped the instant she laid eyes on Hamish Ellerby.

She seemed to stare straight through him.

Hamish felt himself shiver. He was almost relieved when

his mum grabbed him by the scruff of his neck and pulled him quickly down the corridor towards Mrs Quip's room.

He couldn't be sure, but had that baby been holding . . . a baby blue *spanner*?

What's a Tummy Chicken?

Hamish had seen some pretty weird stuff in his ten years on Earth, but he'd never seen a baby with a spanner, or another play the bongos on a pensioner's head.

But then Hamish didn't know that much about babies. Perhaps they were super into DIY and world music. He wouldn't know; he'd never been a big brother. Jimmy was five years older than him. And, to be honest, Hamish didn't find babies that interesting. Once, he had had to do a school project about babies. He'd tried interviewing one and it had gone terribly. He just couldn't get a straight answer out of it. It wouldn't even say if it was a boy or a girl!

In the end – because Hamish loves a list – all he could come up with was this:

1) You never see a baby with a wristwatch.

2) You never hear a baby whistling.

3) Babies are very secretive. They will give up almost no information. They would make fantastic spies.

4) Don't bother asking a baby if it wants a sandwich.

5) Babies seem to have little to no interest in hobbies.

6) A lot of babies stink.

But perhaps babies using spanners and power tools and so on was just something that happened in life, and no one had thought to tell him. He would add it to his list!

Right now, though, Hamish was BORED! He was a good kid, but going to see other people's random babies was not on his **100 Things to Do Before I'm 92** list.

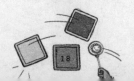

And while Mrs Quip was very nice, with rosy-red cheeks and the hair of an opera singer, she didn't half like talking about baby Boffo. As far as Hamish could tell, Boffo had never actually done anything worth talking about. He'd just been born and then lay there, staring at the ceiling, making cooing noises. Was he a baby or a pigeon? Hamish's mum kept saying how handsome Boffo was, and Boffo didn't even have the good manners to say, 'Thank you, madam!' or, 'I can't take all the credit for that!'

Perhaps, between you and me, all babies are simply naturally arrogant.

'You just missed QUITE a tantrum!' laughed Mrs Quip, as Hamish quietly picked up a copy of the 𝔉rinkley 𝔖tarfish.

It was quite thick. There always seemed to be more news in Frinkley than in Starkley. In fact, the paper's slogan was:

More news than you get in Starkley!

There was a photo of a pale and scared-looking lady with haunted eyes, under the headline:

NURSE PHILATELY PICKERNOSE RETIRES IMMEDIATELY OPENS KEBAB SHOP.

Apparently, she'd named the shop KEBABARET! and it combined her twin loves of kebabs and dance. In the photo, she was standing on her medical skateboard, trying to look happy. But anyone who knew her would tell you that, no matter how much she pretended she'd moved on, this was a woman who missed those babies.

The next story was . . .

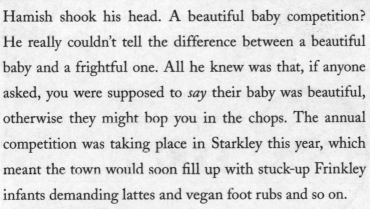

FRINKLEY BABIES SET FOR VICTORY AT REGIONAL BEAUTIFUL BABY COMPETITION!

Hamish shook his head. A beautiful baby competition? He really couldn't tell the difference between a beautiful baby and a frightful one. All he knew was that, if anyone asked, you were supposed to *say* their baby was beautiful, otherwise they might bop you in the chops. The annual competition was taking place in Starkley this year, which meant the town would soon fill up with stuck-up Frinkley infants demanding lattes and vegan foot rubs and so on.

'**DELIVERY!**' yelled a deliverywoman, suddenly shoving her head round the door. She was pulling a huge red cylinder of something marked 'FORMULA ONE'.

'Ooh, thank you,' replied Mrs Quip , delighted. She turned

to Hamish's mum. 'We're getting through this stuff so fast! I won a year's supply from the 𝔉𝔯𝔦𝔫𝔨𝔩𝔢𝔶 𝔖𝔱𝔞𝔯𝔣𝔦𝔰𝔥. There's a whole garage-full at home, plus what they give me here. Boffo can't get enough of it! And it's meant to be so good for him. I can already see the difference!'

Hamish wasn't all that interested in the microscopic differences between one baby and the next. To him, they all looked like little pink balloons someone had drawn a face on. He just smiled to show he was pleased for Mrs Quip as she started to load Formula One into Boffo's bottle. It smelled like cinnamon.

He turned the page of the newspaper to see . . .

EEK!

Well, *that* was one terrifying lady! She had a face like thunder and a hairstyle that looked as if it had been set with a jelly mould. And look what she'd written!

FIVE REASONS WHY FRINKLEY IS BETTER THAN STARKLEY

by Horatia Snipe

It's not boring.
It's not boring.
It's not boring.
Starkley's boring, though.
But Frinkley's not.

Hamish didn't understand why Frinkley was always making fun of Starkley these days. It was his home, and, yes, SURE, it had a reputation for being boring, but most people didn't know the real Starkley. Just imagine if they did!

The real Starkley – the one Hamish couldn't talk about – was a magical place, with a past that could turn your hair white. Oh, Hamish wished he could tell these Frinkley dingbats the secrets of his hometown and set them straight.

He would tell them all about the evil and sinister Axel Scarmarsh, who really seemed to have it in for Starkley.

He would point out the deep black scratch marks that still lined some of the walls in town – the only remaining evidence of the invasion of the fearsome, clawed Terribles who'd tried to steal all the grown-ups and turn them mean.

He'd show them the scuffs on his living-room ceiling – and the tomato-sauce stains – caused by the very first GravityBurp that hit Starkley just two months before. What a day that had been, when everyone's vases and tellies and macaroni pizzas had all shot straight up in the air at once!

And who had fought off all these threats from Scarmarsh? Or the Terribles? Or the ghastly alien overlords, the Superiors?

Not people from Frinkley. No way. It was Hamish Ellerby and his pals in the **Pause Defence Force (PDF).**

And, now that Hamish thought about it, wasn't it Horatia Snipe who had written a really mean article, saying that the

PDF had made all their adventures up? Yes! She'd said Hamish and his pals were 'fantasists', and that they should really be concentrating on their schoolwork instead.

Why had the newspaper recently turned on them?

Maybe Frinkley was just jealous. Okay, it had Laser Quest and a super-cool roundabout with a giant hedge shaped like the wrestler Mr Massive in it. But I ask you: had Frinkley ever been overrun by giant, snapping Venus spytraps? Did it have a shop as cool as **Madame Cous Cous's International World of Treats?**

No, it did not!

Hamish turned to the back page of the paper and found their terrible weekly cartoon, Mr Elbows.

Mr Elbows gave the elbow to Starkley nearly every week. And it was never funny!

Hamish rolled his eyes and put the paper down. Horatia Snipe. Mr Elbows. What was their problem? he wondered. Which was when he noticed that someone was staring at him.

In his cot, little Boffo Quip was sitting bolt upright.

He was still all wrapped up in his muslin, with his minuscule arms strapped tight across his chest, like he was in some kind of baby straitjacket.

But his head was turned and his eyes were boring into Hamish.

Hamish frowned and looked at the grown-ups. They hadn't noticed. Was this normal? Boffo was a newborn. Sitting up seemed rather advanced. And why was he staring at Hamish? It was a bit eerie.

'Hello,' Hamish whispered, because it seemed rude not to say something.

Boffo Quip started to smile. A smile that grew broader and broader.

A toothless, gummy smile.

That sprreeeeead and sprrreeeeead and sprrrrreeeeeeeeead.

And then his nostrils flared.

And there was a low, terrifying **gr000oowwwwl.**

Hamish narrowed his eyes. He and the baby stared at each other for what seemed an eternity.

'Hamish?' said Mum, breaking the spell. 'Is that your tummy, chicken?'

Chicken is what Mum often called Hamish. She wasn't asking if he had a tummy chicken. I have to be honest, I don't even know what a tummy chicken is, but it sounds terrifying. Let's just hope that one day there won't be a book called *Hamish and the Tummy Chickens*.

'That was a highly disgusting growly sound that tells me you must be hungry, love,' said Mum, picking up the 𝔉𝔯𝔦𝔫𝔨𝔩𝔢𝔶 𝔖𝔱𝔞𝔯𝔣𝔦𝔰𝔥 and finding the advert for the local taxi firm, Sharm! Cars. It was called that because they all drove so quickly all you ever heard was shaaaaarm! as they passed. 'Maybe we can stop at Lord of the Fries on the way home.'

But even the promise of chips and battered sausage with mushy peas and curry sauce could not pull Hamish's gaze from this strange, growling baby.

And that was when Hamish Ellerby first suspected that another adventure might be coming.

Hamish Was No Fool!

Hamish Ellerby was no fool. Not on your nelly!

As he arrived home with his battered sausage, he had to consider the evidence that something out of the ordinary was happening.

Babies don't growl.

He'd trained himself to look for anything out of the ordinary these days, just the way a spy spots a lie, a police officer spots a crime or a butcher spots a dodgy sausage.

Mind you, that didn't mean he was never wrong about stuff. He'd seen a cat carrying a deflated balloon in its mouth the other day and convinced himself that the feline world was working on basic flight technology.

'Takeaway again?' asked his brother Jimmy, delighted, nicking one of Hamish's chips. 'You've got to admit, that's the one good thing about Dad being away!'

Hamish's dad worked for a company called **Belasko**.

It was a company with one of those names that didn't really give away very much about what it did. Mainly because what it did was **super-top-secret.**

Or at least it used to be.

The fact was, these days everybody in Starkley knew precisely what **Belasko** was. They knew it was Earth's best hope against whatever evil might come knocking. But they also knew it was no good having a secret organisation if it wasn't secret. Some people from **Belasko** might have been worried that everyone would start talking. They would have gone to the stock cupboard and brought out a **Hypnobit**. But Hamish's dad didn't want to use that little chirruping robot to wipe people's memories. He didn't think that was fair any more. So instead he'd called the whole town together outside the town clock one night and made them take the Starkley Oath. Everyone had to put their hands on their hearts and promise to keep quiet and just carry on and whatnot.

And, now that Hamish was a junior **Belasko** member, he was in the loop; right now, he knew his dad was leading a team of agents out on a mission into **SPACE** – yes, **SPACE!** – to make sure that their old enemy Axel Scarmarsh and the Superiors really had gone away. Dad had

found some clues that led him to believe the evil Superiors were leaving Earth alone for a while.

The question was: why? And where exactly in the universe was Scarmarsh now?

Still, Dad being away on a mission had two distinct advantages:

1. Mum said they could get takeaway from Lord of the Fries, Lord of the Wings or the new place, Thai Robot, whenever they fancied it. Even if that was five times a day and all anyone wanted was a pickled onion.

2. Hamish's dad had given him and his friends a very special job . . .

'You're in charge of Starkley while I'm away,' he'd said, right before he left. 'Keep your eyes peeled. If anything strange occurs, you let me know – but *only if you're absolutely certain*!

We can't risk any more false alarms!'

And there had been quite a few 'false alarms' lately, Hamish would be too embarrassed to tell you. Because of everything that had happened in Starkley, he knew it was his vital duty to keep his eyes peeled for suspicious activity.

The problem is, sometimes that meant he saw it everywhere.

Just this month, Hamish had mistaken a smaller boy at school for an alien shapeshifter (it turned out he'd just changed into his PE kit).

Plus, he'd called out an entire **Belasko** SWAT team when he became convinced that someone had made all the grown-ups disappear suddenly, but he hadn't realised it was Free Pie Night at the Queen's Leg. Everyone was queuing up for beef and onion, and the landlord really didn't appreciate **Belasko** special ops suddenly crashing through his roof.

Dad putting his faith in Hamish now was a big deal. Not just because of the false alarms, but because he was always so protective of his son.

'He just loves you to the moon and back,' his mum always told Hamish. 'He couldn't bear anything happening to you.'

Hamish loved Dad the same way. But this need to always protect Hamish could be frustrating too, because it meant sometimes his dad wouldn't let him take the risks that a real **Belasko** agent had to take. How was he supposed to save the world in a hurry if he had to ask permission first?

Hamish's mum always knew when this was playing on his mind. She'd been rather shocked to find out that her husband was a **super-top-secret agent** instead of a salesman, but something about it just seemed to make sense. He always wore black, for one thing. He was forever buying the latest gadgets. And every time he watched a James Bond film he'd write down the little jokes that James made, just in case he ever found himself in a similar situation.

Jimmy hadn't been all that bothered either, but that was because he was fifteen and fifteen-year-olds are too 'mature' to be fussed about their mum or dad's job.

But, one night a little while ago, Mum had decided to explain to Hamish why his dad was so protective of him.

'Look at this photo,' she'd said, opening up a dusty old

album and immediately spilling Mustn't grumble biscuit crumbs on it. 'Doesn't Dad look like you in this one?'

Hamish's dad was about ten in the photo. He was standing in a loch with a fishing rod, next to another slightly older boy. A thin boy with wavy hair.

'Who's that?' Hamish had asked.

'Dad always says you remind him of him,' Mum replied, with a small smile. 'That's dad's brother. It's a sad story.'

'A sad story?' Hamish had said. 'Why? What happened?'

But Dad had overheard from the next room.

'No time for sad stories!' he'd said, bounding in and scooping away the album. 'Not when we can watch Star Wars instead!'

Dad had given Mum a look just then. Hamish remembered it as a sort of sad shake of the head.

'Hey, H?' said Jimmy, suddenly appearing in front of Hamish and interrupting the memory. 'I've just completed my latest epic poem?'

Jimmy said everything as if he was asking a question. He wasn't someone you'd ask for advice or directions, because he never sounded quite sure of anything.

'But don't ask me to read it to you?' continued Jimmy. 'Because a great artist does not write poems just because he wants to read them out?'

'Okay, Jimmy,' said Hamish, scoffing a chip. 'I will definitely not ask you to do that.'

'Oh . . . but because you seem so interested I'll do it just this once?' said Jimmy, whipping out his pad. 'This piece is called ONCE I WAS A BABY? And it's all about how once I was a baby?'

He cleared his throat and began.

ONCE I WAS A BABY?

by Jimmy Ellerby?

Once i was a baby?
That came out of a lady?
That lady was my mother?
She also had my brother?

But now i am my own man?
With facial hair and suntan?
And one day i'll be older?
Like a really mouldy boulder?

He looked especially pleased with himself about the mouldy boulder line, even though it didn't make sense.

'It's imagery?' he said. 'Like the moss on an old stone? But that wouldn't rhyme, so I said "really mouldy boulder"?'

'It's genius,' lied Hamish, and Jimmy looked really proud. 'Also, all that stuff about being a baby once and then having a brother, that's all true, which makes it very powerful.'

'Thank you, Hamish?' said Jimmy.

Hamish knew the best thing to do with Jimmy was be encouraging and use words like 'genius'. And not to point out that Jimmy didn't have a suntan at all and barely any facial hair.

'Right, I'd better not be late!' said Hamish, checking his watch, **The Explorer**. 'Back in a bit!'

As Hamish walked through the town square, he was excited to be going somewhere very special for a 6 p.m. meeting. But he couldn't get the weirdness of the hospital visit out of his mind.

And it was funny, but he'd never really noticed how many babies there actually were in the world. Now Boffo had given him the heebie-jeebies, he noticed they were **EVERYWHERE.**

He remembered from his school project that something like four babies are born every second.

That's, like, four now!

And another four!

We're already up to twelve!

Now sixteen!

So I suppose it makes sense that they were *all over the place*. I mean, where else would you put them?

But, here in Starkley, Hamish had never really looked at the town's babies. He shrugged and decided that you only really see them when you look for them. Babies blend in. Buggies are just part of the scenery. Mums and dads must almost feel invisible when they're standing behind one.

And, if you do spot a baby, man . . . those parents look so droopy. Clutching their paper cups of coffees and nodding at other parents, or splayed out on park benches, staring at their phones with their baggy eyes while their babies drift off to sleep.

Except how do you know if they're sleeping if you're chatting to other parents, or staring at your phone? Those babies could be up to almost anything. They could be knitting. Or using a soldering iron. Or drawing pictures of bottoms.

For the first time, Hamish saw a whole world of babies: quietly there. Lying down out of sight in their own little vehicles.

The thought made his heart quicken.

He tried to put babies out of his mind and upped his pace.

The others would be waiting in their brand-new, super-exciting headquarters.

Garage 5

The **PDF's** new HQ was a masterpiece of engineering.

Oh, it was a real step up, all right. It was *ridiculously* cool.

In the old days, they'd had to make do with an old shed in the woods.

Then Elliot – the gang's resident genius – had installed a sophisticated **WAR ROOM** at the end of his garden, complete with drawing board and mini-fridge.

But, since they'd proved themselves not once, not twice, but an incredible *three* times, Belasko had decided these were kids with a bright future in the organisation. Kids they should look after.

And so Garage 5 of Slackjaw's Motors had been assigned to the **PDF.**

Slackjaw's Motors, of course, had a secret. The whole town did. If you knew the right people with the right keys, and you knew where to put those keys, you could turn the whole

town upside down . . . almost literally!

But that's a story for another day (and another book). For now, all you need to know is that right here, at this simple car lot, strange flashing lights had been spotted night after night. Some people thought it must have been due to an illegal disco. Others said UFOs. No one had known it was two welders called Barry kitting the place out for the kids.

From the outside, it looked just like a normal garage, with a door painted British Racing Green.

But inside . . . ?

Well . . .

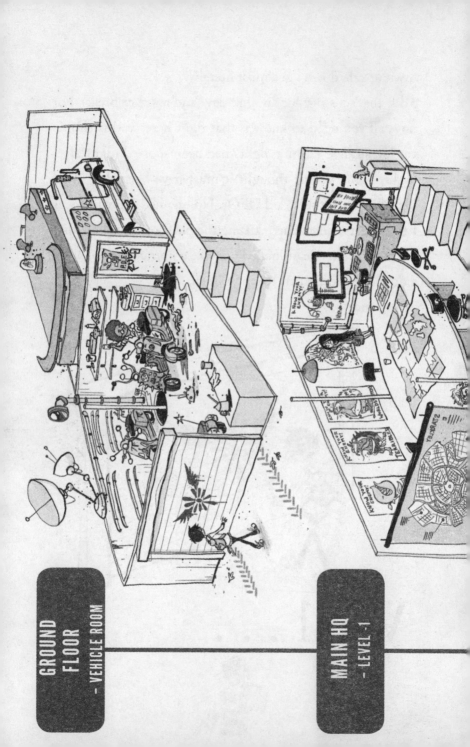

GROUND
FLOOR
– VEHICLE ROOM

MAIN HQ
– LEVEL -1

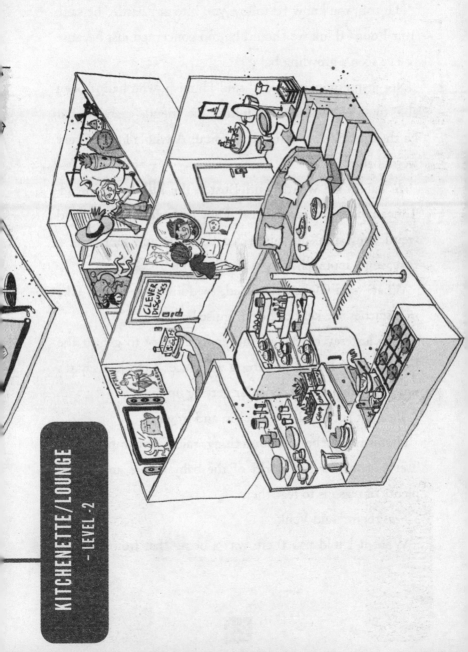

KITCHENETTE/LOUNGE
— LEVEL -2

At the meeting table, chewing an apple, Venk was uncertain.

'Hamish, you know I'd follow you into any battle,' he said. 'But I don't think we should be too concerned just because you've seen a growling baby.'

'Not just a growling baby,' said Hamish, who hadn't been able to stop himself from telling his friends exactly what he thought he'd seen at the hospital. 'A whole load of very weird babies.'

'*All* babies are weird,' said Buster, the **PDF'S** tech-head. 'I mean, have you seen them? They look weird, they sound weird, they speak in this weird language and they have a *very* weird approach to personal hygiene.'

'What?' said Clover, confused, twiddling one of the fake moustaches she kept in her disguise box.

'Let's just say babies are never in a hurry to get to the toilet,' added Buster, making a wise face. 'Let's just say it's not something they'd consider getting up for.'

Alice put her hand on her chin and frowned.

'Hamish might be onto something,' said Elliot, importantly. 'Let us consider the world of the baby. There are indeed plenty of reasons to fear them.'

'*Fear* them?' said Venk.

'What if I told you there was a being that from its very

first moment on Earth had a grip so **POWERFUL** that it could **HANG IN MID-AIR** from a tree like a **BAT** if it wanted?'

Buster looked a little concerned as Elliot put on his most important voice.

'An entity that possessed the immediate ability to SWIM without ever even setting *foot* inside a leisure centre?' he said, placing one hand on Clover's shoulder and making her jump. 'That had a history of breathing underwater? Born with *more bones* than us? *Ten thousand taste buds!* And . . .' – he paused – *'NO KNEECAPS!'*

'Ew!' yelled Venk. 'Like a bony, hungry jellyfish!'

'But wait!' said Elliot. 'An enemy that could move among us *undetected*! And that pees, according to the most recent national statistics, *once every twenty minutes!*'

'Enough!' said Buster. 'I can't hear any more about these fearsome beasts!'

Elliot pressed a button and a screen lowered from the ceiling.

On it was a photograph of a lovely, smiling baby holding a flower.

'Behold the beast!' Elliot announced.

'*Babies?!*' said Alice. 'It just doesn't seem very likely that they'd be a threat.'

Buster nodded.

'I mean, I'm totally on your side, Hamish,' he said, 'but does the phrase "false alarm" mean anything to you? They still haven't repaired the roof of the Queen's Leg yet!'

Hamish blushed.

'Look,' he replied. 'I know that I've got a few things wrong recently, but maybe we can just keep an eye on the babies? We've been put in charge of Starkley while the older agents are away. It's up to us to protect the town . . . to protect the world, even. What if Scarmarsh strikes again?'

The **PDF** considered his words. They knew all too well that their old enemy had been a little quiet of late.

The last time they'd actually seen him had been in London, when he'd blasted off into space using the top of the famous Post Office Tower as his ship. Scarmarsh was an awful man, with dark thoughts and a darker temper, who'd tricked the **PDF** and used Hamish as bait to lure his dad out of hiding so he could zap him.

He'd failed, thank goodness, but failure only makes a baddie badder. It gnaws away at them, reminding them they're not all-powerful, forcing them to try and prove themselves again and again.

The gang didn't want to believe he was still a threat. After all, Hamish was always worried about something or other these days, wasn't he? But still the thought unnerved them.

Scarmarsh, with his terrifying glare . . .

Scarmarsh, who seemed to haunt Hamish's dreams . . .

Scarmarsh, who could look right through you . . .

As Alice always said – you had to be prepared.

'Well, Hamish,' said Elliot. 'If you say there are weird babies out there, who are we to say there aren't?'

'So you'll help me check it out?'

'Of course we will,' said Alice. 'Tomorrow morning, the **PDF** will leave Garage 5 and go and spy on babies.'

When she put it that way, it sounded absolutely ridiculous.

But Hamish knew Alice didn't think it was ridiculous.

And, before you know it, neither will you.

6

Mission Improbable

'Right,' said Venk, turning up slightly late the next morning. 'Let the baby spying begin!'

'Baby spying' didn't sound like the most exciting mission in the world. It was right up there with trouser spotting or lamp staring. But it certainly seemed like one of the easiest.

Because as they stood in Starkley town square and looked across it – all really looked, together – it seemed there were babies absolutely everywhere.

It turns out you don't really need to spy on babies. Babies are terrible at hiding.

It was a Saturday morning, so older brothers and sisters were watching cartoons, or at sports practice, or at their friend's house, or riding their bike. It was just babies everywhere. Buggies littered the square. Distracted parents sat nearby.

'What is this?' said Venk. 'International Baby Week?'

'Let's just have a gentle stroll,' said Hamish.

'How do we know a "good" baby from a "weird" one?' said Buster. 'Like I said, every one of them's a weirdo.'

Infants sat on the grass, staring at flowers.

Mums and dads gently rocked prams as they stared at their phones.

It seemed a perfectly pleasant Starkley morning. The sun was shining and the sound of gentle laughter filled the air.

It was all just perfectly . . . pleasant.

'So are you, um, sure about this?' said Alice, trying to look ready for action. 'Only I'm not really sensing any real sort of threat here.'

'Just wait,' said Hamish. 'They'll start beating people up or pushing them through doors soon.'

Buster and Venk swapped a worried glance. They'd been through a lot with Hamish – they wanted to believe him – but this did sound a bit odd.

Hamish could sense their growing doubt. It irritated him, if he was honest. The last time he'd felt like this was when his dad had tried to stop him from getting too involved in saving the world – even though, when the GravityBurps hit Starkley, it had been Hamish who had led the way.

He'd always been a bit frustrated when his dad kept trying to keep him out of things. But now he understood a bit more.

You see, after he'd seen the photo of Dad and his brother, Hamish hadn't been able to stop thinking about it and had tried to speak to Dad about it. He'd never thought to ask before if his dad had brothers or sisters. He'd just assumed that because he didn't know about them, he couldn't have.

But Dad didn't want to talk about it. He had a way of changing the subject. Always cheerfully, of course, and suggesting some distraction, like a kickabout in the garden, or a new film to watch. But Hamish had started to feel that sometimes people might pretend to be cheerful to hide a sadness within. He could tell whatever it was his dad was hiding was pretty big, or pretty sad. At first he was disappointed that there were more secrets being kept from him, but over hot chocolate one night, Mum revealed a little more.

She said Dad really didn't like to talk about his brother or what had happened between them. She told Hamish that when Angus Ellerby was a kid – maybe just a little older than Jimmy was now – he'd shared a room with his brother, Al, on the farm in Scotland.

Al was a little older than Angus. They were inseparable and used to play for hours down in the wetlands. The boys would fish, whittle wood, and learned how to start a fire with nothing more than a couple of pieces of old flint. It was like basic **Belasko** recruit training. And then they'd run by the wetlands, or on the coastal salt marshes. Beside wet dune slacks and woodlands. Past swamps and blanket bogs. By river valleys and loch edges.

The boys used to play by these, even though Hamish's grandparents told them not to.

It was dangerous! they'd say. They could get stuck! Or contract some horrible disease in those muck-filled breeding grounds for pests!

But the boys did it anyway; they'd run through clouds of midges, dodging dragonflies and looking for mussels in freshwater rivers.

Life had been fun. The Ellerby boys made sure of it.

And then the clouds came. It was winter. And, on the day they were sitting in a tree over the marshes, Angus did something he would regret forever.

He pushed his brother, just for a joke. Just to scare him. The way they both always scared each other as kids do.

But his brother had been caught off guard. He thought they'd stopped playing. He wasn't ready and he fell.

There was a rock down below, hidden just beneath the surface of the swamp . . .

'HAMISH!' said Alice, suddenly, shaking his shoulder and bringing him back from his thoughts. 'Do you feel that?'

It certainly felt a little colder. It was like he'd brought the darkening clouds from his imagination into real life. The wind rose ever so slightly. And as it did . . .

. . . *a lone baby seemed to slowly rise from its slumber.*

'Look,' said Hamish, sensing something unusual. 'What's that little guy doing?'

The baby had a strange fixed grin. It lowered

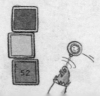

its head but kept staring their way.

Its arms began to rise . . . and it pointed straight at them.

'Okay, that's very creepy,' said Buster, taking a step back.

But the creepiness was just beginning.

As the air grew colder and the trees loudly swayed, another baby shot bolt upright in its pram.

Then another!

They both pointed at the **PDF**, as the wind rose and swept and whipped.

'What's going on?' cried Elliot. **'Why are all these creepy babies pointing at us?'**

'Why aren't their parents doing anything?' said Clover.

But, oh my gosh, look at the parents . . .

They were blank-eyed. Their knuckles seem to drag on the ground, their shoulders sagging from carrying heavy changing bags and shopping. Some trudged slowly around the square, dragging their legs behind them and barely talking, just grunting at each other.

They looked brainwashed.

'Are they . . . *zombies?*' whispered Clover, as one slowly passed by, mumbling to herself.

'No,' said Alice. 'They're just *exhausted.*'

Of course!

The babies had probably kept their parents up all night. Wailing, shouting, screaming and ultra-pooping.

But what was causing the babies to act so oddly?

And why were they suddenly so scary?

'Okay, just . . . keep . . . moving,' whispered Alice through gritted teeth. 'Let's get back to base. Don't . . . make . . . any sudden movements.'

'**Look!**' said Buster.

Up ahead was a new father with a handlebar moustache. He was wearing a baby sling on his chest.

'**La la la la la!**' he sang, happily, and completely out of tune.

He looked strangely out of place. Full of beans. Pleased with himself. And very prepared for fatherhood. He had trousers with enormous pockets packed with milk bottles, nappies and wipes, and this grown-up was now whistling in a carefree manner and patting his sleeping baby.

But he hadn't noticed that his 'sleeping' baby was suddenly wide awake.

It peeked out from the man's chest and spotted Hamish and Alice . . . then two small arms reached upwards.

The dad couldn't believe what was happening. His tiny child had grabbed his moustache and wouldn't let go.

'**OW!**' yelled the man, as the baby began to tug on it. '**OW!**'

This was a baby who knew what she was doing.

Whenever she yanked left, her dad would shout, '**Ow!**' and stumble left.

If she yanked right, her dad would stumble right.

At this precise moment, the baby was pulling as hard as she could – weaving her dad straight towards Hamish and Alice.

'Look out!' said Hamish, horrified. 'He's got hot coffee!'

The dad's steaming drink was teetering in his hand, and spilling its boiling contents every time he changed direction.

He was spinning right the way around now, trying to bat his child's hand off his moustache with his free hand.

'**NO! Pepperino! Release Papa!**'

But this baby was an expert driver!

A simple kick to the tummy made her dad bend over, which was particularly handy for getting through low doors.

And, if she pulled really hard, her dad would speed up.

Her dad was just a horse to her . . .

Now this poor man was hurtling straight at Hamish and Alice – his boiling hot coffee coming right for them!

'**JUMP!**' yelled Hamish, pushing Alice into a bush.

The dad and his baby shot past.

The baby tried to spin her dad around with a powerful tug of his moustache, but they were going too quickly.

Still careering backwards, the man's bottom hit a bin and he fell straight in. He was stuck fast!

His furious, upside-down baby started punching him in the face!

'Let's get out of here!' said Venk, but it was no good – they were still right in the middle of the square. Babies crawled slowly around them, like tigers stalking their prey.

'Surrounded,' said Alice, adopting a karate pose.

'What are you going to do?' asked Venk, amazed. 'Fight a baby?'

'We fell right into their trap,' said Hamish, frustrated with himself.

More heads popped out of prams and buggies.

Some wearing bonnets.

Some in tiny baseball caps.

Still the other tiger-babies prowled on all fours, their heads suddenly snapping round to keep a beady eye on Hamish and his friends.

Nostrils flaring. Growling.

'Don't make eye contact,' said Hamish, quivering. 'Show no fear.'

'Just be confident,' said Alice, as Hamish gripped her hand. 'They're just babies, remember. They're **JUST. BABIES!'**

And then one of those babies got to its feet and started to run straight towards Alice.

'Aaaargh!' she screamed, as it leapt high into the air, and . . .

'RAAAAAAWRRL!'

7

Thar He Blows!

Hamish and the **PDF** threw open the door of 13 Lovelock Close in a screaming panic and slammed it shut behind them.

Alice, Buster, Venk, Elliot and Clover thundered up the stairs to Hamish's room while Hamish, out of breath, pressed his nose against the window in the hall and made sure they hadn't been followed by any terrifying babies.

Yep. That's a pretty embarrassing sentence . . .

But they'd managed to escape that last one as it broke away from the pack by leaping over the small fence around the flower beds. The baby had slammed straight into it, growling and barking and snapping its gums at them as they legged it away. It would have kept coming after them if it hadn't been on baby reins.

The **PDF** had run to Hamish's house instead of Garage 5 because at least there'd be grown-ups around. Grown-ups

they could warn about what looked like the beginnings of an infant uprising!

They gibbered and jabbered at each other as they slammed Hamish's bedroom door shut. It seemed to have affected *every baby in town.*

'Hamish?' yelled his mum. 'What's all the noise?'

Hamish double-locked the front door then ran to the living room.

'MUM!' he said, but stopped in his tracks as he saw a horrifying sight.

A dreadful sight!

Mum had *visitors*!

'Look,' said Mum, delighted, holding out her teacup. 'It's Mrs Quip and Boffo!'

Hamish almost didn't recognise Boffo at first.

He seemed to have gained rather a lot of weight since Hamish had first seen him. He was really rather hefty. He had chubby little arms that looked like a row of bread rolls. Fat little fingers like sausages. He looked like a baby Emperor, sitting there on the sofa, all pompous.

'Oh . . . er, hi, Boffo,' said Hamish, trying to stay calm. How could he talk to Mum now?

Boffo Quip was frowning and staring at him, as if he was trying to read Hamish's mind. He had tearstains on his cheeks. Evidently, he'd just had another Mega Boffo Tantrum.

Even though Boffo was a newborn, he appeared to already be on solids. Specifically, he was halfway through his second pack of Hamish's mum's chocolate Mustn'tgrumbles. That was probably the only way they'd stopped him crying and yelling. I know that's what happens with me.

Hamish studied the little man more closely.

Was that . . . the beginning of a *moustache*?

Boffo was barely three weeks old and already he was more manly than Jimmy. This was extremely odd.

'We're thinking of entering Boffo into the Beautiful Baby Competition,' said Mrs Quip, cooing over him. 'Though we'll probably wait until he looks a little less grumpy!'

But Boffo didn't just look grumpy. He looked *furious*.

Hamish didn't know what to do. He'd run home to get away from babies, and now there was one right here in his own living room, scoffing his mum's biscuits!

'Why don't you sit down next to him, Hamish?' asked Mum.

'Uh, no, thanks,' said Hamish. 'I've got my friends round, and—'

'I'm sure they can wait a few minutes?' said Mum. 'Come and sit down!'

Hamish smiled nervously, then very slowly and cautiously sat down next to Boffo. He perched as far away from him as he could. He didn't like the look of this baby one bit. Boffo was staring at him and breathing heavily, like a dog you wouldn't trust.

Hamish noticed Boffo had a weird pink teddy bear with him. He'd seen these advertised on TV. It was called **TOPPY SPARKLES**. It had the biggest, strangest googly eyes and a rainbow-coloured tummy. And it had cheap glitter on its cheeks, which kept falling off. Anyone who came within three metres of Toppy Sparkles ended up with glitter on them somehow. Mum's face was already covered in it. She looked like she was auditioning for *Balldancing Fever!* but for the part of the disco ball in the opening titles.

To sum up, Toppy Sparkles was a very creepy teddy bear.

If you pushed its nose, it yelled, **'I'M TOPPY SPARKLES!'** far too loudly in a Chinese accent. If you wanted it to *stop* shouting, **'I'M TOPPY**

SPARKLES!', you were out of luck. You just had to wait until it finished. It could go on for hours. Lots of parents had tried to get it banned, because every night, all over Britain, mums or dads putting toys away would accidentally tread on their Toppy Sparkles and the whole street would be up all night listening to **'I'M TOPPY SPARKLES! I'M TOPPY SPARKLES! I'M TOPPY SPARKLES!'** over and over.

'Would you like to hold Boffo, Hamish?' asked Mrs Quip, suddenly.

Would he like to hold him? Look at the size of him! How would Hamish even pick him up?!

'Oh, I'd worry about dropping him,' said Hamish, even though if you dropped this baby you'd be more worried about damaging the floor. The aftershocks would go on for weeks. They'd be felt in China.

'You'll be fine!' said Mrs Quip, grinning encouragingly. 'Go on, have a cuddle!'

'No, thanks, Mrs Quip,' said Hamish.

Boffo's eyes widened as he took an enormous, massive breath.

'WAAAAAAH!'

he screamed.

It was a deafening cry.

'See?' said Mrs Quip. 'He wants you to pick him up!'

Boffo immediately stopped.

'Um, okay,' said Hamish.

'Oof,' she said. 'Watch out, he's a big'un . . .'

She dropped him onto Hamish's lap. Boffo's heels dug straight in and Hamish's eyes started to water, because that was one place boys don't like to be kicked.

Close up, Boffo stared at Hamish.

His baby breath was sour with a hint of . . . cinnamon?

Hamish didn't like the way Boffo was looking at him. It felt like at any second this baby might do something crazy and unpredictable. But he c ouldn't let on to the grown-ups. Not in front of Boffo. He felt instinctively that Boffo would not appreciate that one bit.

'You should be careful, actually,' said Mrs Quip. 'He's just had rather a lot of formula to drink.'

Ah, that would explain the cinnamon smell.

'Um, why do you say I should be careful?' asked Hamish, now feeling rather on edge.

'Oh, it's just that sometimes, right after his milk, Boffo might have a little vomit.'

This information did not sit at all well with Hamish.

'A little *vomit?*' he said, as Boffo started to smile.

'Yes, just a little vomit,' said Mrs Quip. 'It's perfectly

normal.'

Boffo kept smiling as Hamish stared into his eyes. They seemed to have changed colour. They were now bright green and Hamish could make out a look of anticipation.

What exactly was this baby planning?

'You can have him back now!' said Hamish, struggling to turn the giant baby. But he could barely lift him to hand him back.

'No, no,' said Mrs Quip. 'You enjoy him!'

'Honestly, take him back!' said Hamish, his arms now shaking from the weight of the baby beast. 'I think you should—'And then he stopped.

Because he could feel a **rumble.**

And the **rumble** became a **VIBRATION**.

And the **VIBRATION** became a SHAKE.

And the SHAKE became—

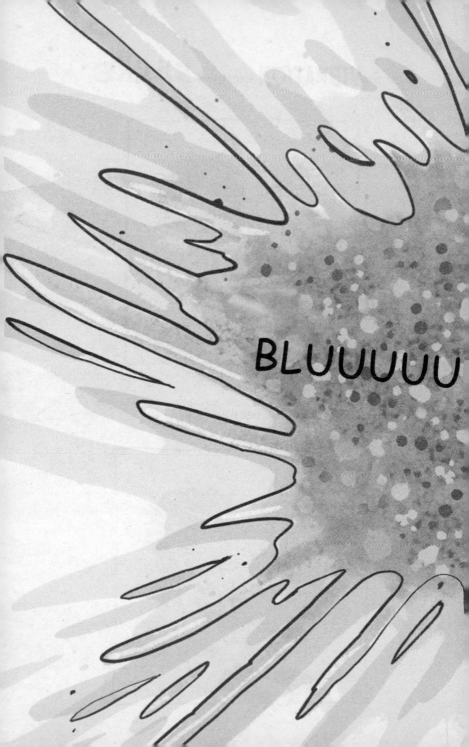

Oh, poor Hamish! A river of milk began to pound his face!

'AAAAAARRRGH!' yelled Hamish

BLUUUUUUUUURRGH! continued Boffo,

who now looked like a milk-dispensing fire extinguisher.

He was bright red and the milk was shooting out fast!

'AAAARGH!' yelled Mum.

'AAAARGH!' yelled Mrs Quip.

BLUUUUUUUUUURGH! continued Boffo.

This was insane! Unstoppable! It was like a firefighter's hose on full blast!

How much milk had this baby *drunk*?

'AAAARGH!' yelled Hamish, still holding him.

BLLUUUUUURGH! continued Boffo.

When would it stop? When would it *stop*?

All Hamish could do was keep the baby in the air and try and point him at places he wouldn't cause too much mess. Hamish was already soaked, so he aimed Boffo at his mum's wellington boots by the door.

And, finally, Boffo stopped. Just like that.

'This is the worst day of my life!' said Hamish – and that was saying something.

BUUUUUUUUUUUUUUUURP

burped Boffo, beaming.

'I've been BABIED!' yelled Hamish, as Mrs Quip tried to wipe his face with a tiny towelette.

'Hamish!' said Alice, standing in the doorway, looking pale. 'We need you upstairs. Fast.'

8

Leg It, Hamish!

In Hamish's room, the **PDF** were all pressed up against the window.

'What is it?' asked Hamish, rushing in and sopping wet.

'What's that *smell?*' said Clover, holding her nose. 'Is that . . . *cinnamon?*'

'I was babied,' said Hamish, appalled. 'It lasted so long that I thought I'd spend the rest of my life being barfed over!'

'Look,' said Buster. 'Here it comes again!'

Hamish walked over to the window and peered outside. All he could see was one of those *Sharm!* cars from Frinkley. Mrs Quip must have ordered it to take them home.

'Over there,' said Buster, pointing. 'On the corner!'

And there, just where Lovelock Close meets Myna Street, a lone pram trundled along the pavement.

Hamish stared for a second before realising what the big deal was . . .

Because, yes. You read that right. *A lone pram.*

It was black, with its hood pulled right down, and it was smoothly coasting down the street, completely on its own, with no parent or big brother or sister to be seen.

'We should stop it,' said Hamish, uncertainly. 'I mean, what do we do? It's a runaway pram!'

'Wait,' said Elliot. 'Watch.'

The pram didn't seem out of control – that was the strange thing. It was maintaining a steady speed. It was going neither slowly nor quickly. It just seemed to be cruising.

'That's the third time it's been down your street, Hamish,' explained Elliot, peeking at it from behind the curtain. 'Now watch this!'

There was dog poo maybe ten metres in front of the pram, right in the middle of the pavement, just outside Mr Ramsface's house. It must have been old Mr Neate's dog that had done it. Old Mr Neate didn't pick up after his dog. He'd say: 'What am I supposed to do with that? Pop it on my head and pretend it's a hat? Make a lovely teapot out of it?'

And people would reply: 'Er, no. You throw it in the special bin.'

And old Mr Neate would walk away, laughing, like they'd just told him a really good joke.

The pram had nearly reached the poo now. By Elliot's calculations, it would be no more than 3.6 seconds before the pram sliced through the dog's awful doings. Hamish held his breath.

And, at the very last moment, the pram *swerved perfectly around it*.

'What the . . . ?' said Hamish, startled and a little afraid.

He'd heard of self-driving cars. But not poo-swerving prams.

Then, once it was past the doo-doo, the pram turned and, as if someone had jammed on the accelerator, it **SHOT OFF** down the street, as a cat jumped out of its way in fright.

'Well, I think it's safe to say something's definitely going on in Starkley,' said Alice, watching it skid round the corner. 'Again.'

'But what?' asked Clover. 'I mean, it's not like these babies have actually done anything.'

'They've pushed people in bins!' said Hamish. 'And flicked their bottoms! And leapt at us and ROARED. What if it's building up to something?'

Hamish heard his front door slam shut. They all watched as Mrs Quip walked down the path to the taxi, clearly struggling under the weight of Boffo.

She strapped him into a baby seat, while the driver sat inside and tried to retune his radio. Well, he kept hitting it. Hamish's mum was waving them off and saying things like, 'And thank you so much for asking! We *love* babies! We'd be so happy to look after him anytime! Hamish will be *delighted*!'

Boffo looked up at Hamish and grinned.

It sent shivers down his spine.

Downstairs, in the kitchen that night, Hamish's mum was humming a happy tune. He was pleased she was happy. Things had been stressful and hectic for her in the Complaints Department of Starkley Town Council recently. Complaints had been flooding in! Though, weirdly, a lot of these complaints were from people living in Frinkley. It was exhausting.

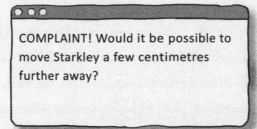

COMPLAINT! Would it be possible to move Starkley a few centimetres further away?

COMPLAINT! If you mix Frinkley with Starkley, you get Stinkley so I think Starkley should change its name.

COMPLAINT! It's been windy lately and I blame Starkley!

Usually around now, Mum would be listening to the Janice Mad Show on Starkley FM. They'd be doing a phone-in about what the weather's like. Was all she ever did, and it was normally just lots of people getting in touch to say exactly the same thing.

'Peter in Starkley says it's cloudy at the moment,' Janice would say, reading out the texts. 'Paul in Starkley says it's cloudy. Pippin in Starkley says it's cloudy. Percy in Starkley says it's quite cloudy at the moment.'

On and on she'd go, never once thinking that all anyone had to do to see what the weather was like was look out of the window. But tonight for some reason the radio was just making a horrible CHHHHHH static noise instead and his mum didn't seem to have noticed.

Hamish switched the radio off and wondered how to raise the idea of psycho babies with her. Particularly as her good friend had apparently just had one. I mean, you can't say that about someone's newborn, can you? You can't say: 'Oh, you appear to have given birth to a terrifying baby!'

'Mum?' said Hamish, edging closer. 'Um, can I ask you something?'

'Yes?'

'It's a bit . . . delicate.'

'Oh!' said his mum. 'Of course, chicken. Anything.'

'It's about . . . babies.'

'Ah,' said Mum, suddenly looking absolutely terrified. She started to move things around on the dinner table which didn't need to be moved around. That was odd. Why would his mum look terrified just because he wanted to ask about babies?

'Hah! You know something, don't you?' Hamish said. 'You know something about babies!'

She went red.

'I thought you knew,' she said, looking anywhere but at her son.

Hamish's eyes widened.

'So . . . it's *true*?' he said. 'And they can control buggies?'

77

His mum stared at him.

'What is it exactly you want to know about babies?' she asked.

'I think they've all gone weird,' he said. 'I'm worried there's more to it.'

'Oh!' said his mum, looking strangely relieved. 'Well, I mean, babies *are* a bit weird.'

'*Too* weird,' said Hamish. 'And, as Protector of Starkley, I'm going to find out why!'

'Well,' she replied, 'you'll have plenty of chances to study one. Mrs Quip has asked if we'd look after Boffo for a few hours here and there this week. And I said of course.'

Hamish suddenly noticed that Mrs Quip had left a vast Formula One tank with a bright red pipe for Boffo to suck on. It gurgled and blurgled in the corner. It was on wheels so it could be carted to wherever the little emperor was. The stench of cinnamon began to sting Hamish's eyes.

Boffo's Formula One tank. In *his* kitchen.

'Wasn't Boffo just a sweetheart?' said Mum. 'Just the cutest? Just the cuddliest?'

Hamish realised he'd be seeing a lot more of Boffo Quip. And that his own mother had been won over by him. What was it with adults and babies? Why couldn't they see what

Hamish did? That babies weren't as cute, small and helpless as they wanted you to believe? Maybe he needed to tell Dad, because Hamish's world was starting to feel smaller. Babies were beginning to take over his thoughts the way one had already started to take over his kitchen.

Was he going crazy, or . . . was this some kind of *invasion*?

Hamish couldn't shake the feeling that he was being targeted.

The Curious Case
of the Bear in
the Night-time

Hamish tried to put all thoughts of being singled out by the babies from his mind. It was silly, wasn't it?

Yes, so babies had gone crazy in the hospital. And yes, they'd gone crazy in the town square. And sure, one had vomited all over him in his own home and left a huge tank of cinnamon-stinking formula in his kitchen, but really – they were just *babies*. Even if they were scary, they were nothing to be afraid of. He could hardly interrupt his dad's mission to track down evil old Scarmarsh and say, 'Please come back to Starkley – there's loads of weird babies!', could he?

No, there was probably a very simple explanation. So Hamish brushed his teeth, washed his face and popped his pyjamas on as usual. He pushed open the door to his bedroom, closed his window, turned his bedside light on and popped a glass of water on his bedside table, just as he always did.

Then, as usual, he said hello to baby Boffo's weird Toppy Sparkles bear that was in his bed and made sure it was all tucked in.

Then he . . .

Wait.

Hang on a second . . . What did I just say?

Hamish stopped in his tracks and took a second look.

Staring out from his bed (now tucked up rather nicely) was a bright blue teddy bear.

'Toppy Sparkles,' Hamish whispered to himself.

But this wasn't Boffo's – his was pink – so whose was it?

Wait. What if . . . Boffo had *been in his room*?

No. That was impossible. How could he have been?

And surely his friends would have noticed if the bear had been there all along.

Hamish's eyes flicked to the window he'd just closed. Had he left that open? Or had Mum?

He eyed the teddy suspiciously as he walked round his bed. Its weird eyes seemed to follow him. Where was he going to put this stuffed monstrosity? He didn't want to wake up in the middle of the night and feel like Toppy Sparkles was staring at him, all googly-eyed and terrifying. Or for Toppy Sparkles to malfunction somehow, and start yelling, **'I'M TOPPY SPARKLES!'** at the top of its voice at two in the morning. Maybe Hamish should stick him in a drawer until he could get rid of the bear in the morning.

Yeah. He'd do that.

Hamish reached to grab Toppy Sparkles, pulled his duvet back ...

And *screamed!*

'AARGH!'

Because, when Hamish really, properly looked at this Toppy Sparkles, all he could see ...

... was its head!

Where was its body? What had happened to poor Toppy Sparkles?!

What kind of monster would do something like this? thought Hamish, flattened against the wall, as Toppy Sparkles' weird googly eyes looked weirder and more googly and deranged than ever. This was horrifying!

Hamish needed air so he went to open his window. And his heart nearly stopped.

Across from him, down on the street by the Ramsface residence, stood a shady and mysterious figure.

Who was that? What were they doing?

A tall man in a wide-brimmed hat and a long brown jacket leaned against a lamp post.

The world seemed suddenly silent, except for the sound of Hamish's own heartbeat throbbing in his ears.

He put his hands flat on the glass to steady himself, and stared out as the stranger looked up and down the street. And then, as if he knew he was being watched, the man looked up . . .

And stared straight at Hamish.

They locked eyes.

The stranger tipped his hat at young Hamish.

Hamish was scared. There was something not right . . .

He wanted to back away from the window and disappear into the relative darkness of his own room, but he was too terrified. For a start, Toppy Sparkles was there.

Or some of him anyway.

The man took a step forward, into the light from the lamp post, and gave Hamish a strange and creepy smile.

Then, right behind the figure, the lights in the Ramsface house suddenly came on.

'All right, all right, I'm DOING it,' came a distant but familiar voice.

It was Mr Ramsface. Obviously unlocking the front door so he could put the bins out.

What would the tall man do now? Walk away?

But what happened was far odder and more heart-jangling than that.

The man in the hat turned round and simply *collapsed in a heap*!

I'm serious. Just like that! Collapsed in a heap!

Hamish watched as the man just crumpled to the ground.

He'd gone from six feet tall to almost nothing in a heartbeart.

All that remained was the coat, the hat and a pair of brown leather shoes on the pavement below.

Hamish was confused. People don't just . . . crumple!

Had the guy fallen into a manhole? Had gravity somehow crushed him to the size of a beef-and-onion Oxo cube? Had he *evaporated*?

And then, as Mr Ramsface finally managed to get his own front door open, Hamish stared in disbelief as the coat gently wriggled on the ground for a second.

Then *four tiny figures* – who Hamish now realised had been standing on each other's shoulders under the coat – popped out from underneath and sped away in different directions under cover of darkness, their tiny hands slapping the pavement.

Hamish put his hand to his mouth. He knew then and there that he'd been sent a message.

The head of Toppy Sparkles.

The tank in the kitchen.

The collapsible baby man.

Hamish been told to Back Off . . .

By a gang of terrifying babies.

Bully For You

It was the next morning and the PDF were up bright and early and pacing around Garage 5.

'They're getting stronger?' said Buster. '*Intimidating* you?'

'I think the buggy followed us from the square after that baby jumped at us,' said Hamish, sitting down at the table. 'And it made sure that was where I lived. And then those other babies were sent to bully me.'

It sounded a bit odd, saying that some babies were bullying him. But that's what it felt like. Hamish had some serious bags under his eyes. He'd barely slept as he kept worrying that a baby would shimmy up the drainpipe and start slapping him awake or tweaking his nose or something.

But what he couldn't work out was why the babies would be targeting him in the first place.

'I've been doing some research!' said Clover, producing a

clipboard and a doll. 'And what I've found out will startle you, confound you and concern you. Gather round!'

She held up the doll with one hand and pointed at it with the other.

'This is a baby,' she said.

The **PDF** all stared at the doll. They didn't need to. They all knew what a baby looked like.

'You can tell it's a baby,' said Clover, 'by its baby face, baby eyes and baby size.'

Elliot looked impressed and made notes.

'But now . . .' said Clover, and she reached into her pocket and took out a golden wig, which she lay across the doll's head, '. . . it's a very small man.'

She put the doll on a chair for everybody to stare at and nodded importantly, like she'd just blown their minds.

The whole team waited for the next part of the presentation.

'So that's it,' said Clover.

'Oh!' said Hamish. 'Well, thank you, Clo. That was very . . . short.'

'So if it's wearing a golden wig,' said Venk, confused, 'it's a very small man . . .'

Clover looked a little embarrassed all of a sudden.

'What Clover means,' said Alice, 'is that we need to be on

our guard. babies are wily. They may use disguises. They can infiltrate society at every level. They can get anywhere, be anyone. Right, Clo?'

'Right!' said Clover. 'That's exactly what I meant.'

Hamish had been working on a plan of his own.

'We need to know where they're coming from, what's causing this and what they want,' Hamish said. His sleepless night had given him plenty of time to start thinking about a plan to find out what on earth was happening. He took a very deep breath.

'We have to go to Frinkley.'

'Frinkley?' said Buster, horrified.

No one on the team wanted to go. I mean, sure, it was glamorous. And yes, that huge wrestler, Mr Massive, had been born there. But you don't want to go where you're not welcome, do you?

Hamish could see from the looks on the **PDF'S** faces that they were not keen.

'Look, all these babies are being born in Frinkley Hospital,' said Hamish. 'It's where I saw the really weird stuff happening.'

'But these babies are too small to be doing all that,' said Buster. 'They're newborns! Or three-month-olds! Even if they're a *year* old, they can't be doing half this nonsense!'

Hamish understood Buster's point exactly.

'Something's going on,' he said. 'And, if there is, we need to do something about it. We need proof.'

'And *then* we tell **Belasko**?' asked Clover.

'Right now,' said Alice, smiling, 'we *are* **Belasko**.'

An hour later, after an inspiring motivational speech from Alice, the gang roared their mopeds past the hospital gates in Frinkley and parked up just out of sight, opposite the luggage shop, Larch Molar's Bags.

Hamish's moped was brand new, due to accidentally having his stolen by a gang of Terribles not long ago. His new moped was called **HOWLER**, and he was pretty proud of it. It was blue and had a big red **H** down the side, plus a go-faster stripe, a small box for sandwiches and a *'Reverse Leopard'* sirenforwhenhereallyneededtoget somewhere in a hurry, or needed to speak to a leopard.

'Why do they need an advert for Frinkley in Frinkley?' said Buster, pointing at a big billboard above them. 'We're already in Frinkley. It's not like people who are already in Frinkley will see the advert for Frinkley and say, "We should go to Frinkley!" They're in Frinkley!'

The advert was certainly very bold. It had a photo of
Mr Massive on it, the local celebrity. He was the star of
the Mr Massive Show and did the voiceover on Europe's
Most Massive Men.

'We need to keep a low profile,' said Alice.

'We're a bunch of ten-year-olds with mopeds,' replied
Venk. 'That might be hard.'

'Wait,' said Clover.

She took off an enormous backpack and opened it up.

Hot dogs in every shoe shop! •••• Birthplace of Mr Ma

'Doctors' uniforms,' she said. 'Stethoscopes. Thermometers. That weird little disc thing you wear on your head ...'

Hamish's plan was simple. Get inside Frinkley Hospital. Find some evidence of weird baby behaviour. Then, as junior agents currently responsible for the local area, get in touch with Hamish's dad and other **Belasko** agents to ask permission to put a stop to it. Because, even though they were still the **PDF**, they were part of something bigger now.

NKLEY!

DID YOU KNOW THAT FRINKLEY IS A GERMAN WORD MEANING 'TOWN THAT ALL NEARBY TOWNS ARE JEALOUS OF'? WELL, IT'S NOT BUT IT COULD BE, COULDN'T IT?

•••• Europe's tallest dustbin! •••• The new potato-recycling centre!

The gang started to quickly pull their doctors' uniforms on over their normal clothes.

'Wait!' said Buster. 'How come my one's different?'

'I didn't have quite enough uniforms,' said Clover, apologetically. 'I'm afraid that's why you have to be an old lady.'

'Me?' said Buster, appalled. He held up a bright green flowery dress. 'Why do I have to be the old lady?'

'You were born in Frinkley,' said Clover. 'One of the doctors might recognise you from when you popped out of your mum. You need a little more disguising!'

'Haha,' said Venk, who you'd never catch for a *second* in an uncool costume. But then his face fell.

Outside the newsagent's was a poster advertising the latest edition of the 𝕱𝖗𝖎𝖓𝖐𝖑𝖊𝖞 𝕾𝖙𝖆𝖗𝖋𝖎𝖘𝖍.

It said:

WHO'S AFRAID OF A BABY? THE PDF!

'Afraid of a baby?' said Alice.

Hamish frowned and strode inside, returning ten seconds later with a copy of the *Starfish*. Everyone gathered round as he flicked through it, and saw, with horror, a whole page about them, complete with a huge photo someone must have snapped on their phone.

BIG
BABIES!

PDF RUN AWAY SCREAMING FROM TINY INFANT!

by Horatia Snipe

Take a look at this picture. That's Hamish Ellerby and Alice Shepherd, the so-called 'leaders' of Starkley's Pause Defence Force.

And do you know what's happening? They're running away from a lovely, friendly baby who just wanted a little cuddle and might have coughed a little too loudly!

The poor, delicate PDF couldn't scarper fast enough!

So much for heroes, eh? HEROES AFRAID OF A BABY!

The truth of the matter is that the PDF are not heroes. If they were really heroes, they'd come from Frinkley! And goodness knows how they'll react later this week when the Beautiful Baby Competition hits Starkley. Maybe the PDF should be the ones wearing nappies!!!

Hamish had read enough. He thrust the newspaper at Elliot.

'Oh, no,' said Elliot, pointing at the back page. 'Even Mr Elbows is having a go at us.'

Hamish fumed. He hated Mr Elbows. He thought Mr Elbows was a right old wally. And this was not fair at all. Hamish wasn't scared of babies. He just had a sneaking suspicion that they might be some kind of threat to national security and world safety.

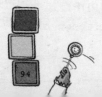

Hamish felt bad that the newspaper was writing this kind of thing about his pals – and all because of him. It made him even more determined to prove to the others that the baby threat was real.

'Oh my GOSH,' whispered Buster as they walked inside the hospital. His eyes were the size of pies. 'They're

EVERYWHERE!'

Ha! thought Hamish. Now the others would see how dangerous babies could be!

Buster was wearing an enormous hat with flowers on, along with his dress, and being pushed in a wheelchair while the rest of the **PDF** pretended to be very busy and concerned doctors, making sure he was okay.

Buster was right, though. There were babies left, right and centre.

Hamish kept a beady eye on them, as parents bent over them, cooing. Some were being strapped into car seats, ready to be driven to waiting cots in Frinkley, Starkley, Thrump, Pilbox and Blund. Others just sat about, breaking wind and smiling.

'So what exactly are we looking for?' Alice asked Hamish.

'Anything unusual,' he said, firmly. 'Let's head for the room where Boffo was.'

Doctors and nurses strode around, deep in conversation, as Hamish led his small gang down the corridor. It felt very naughty being here, even though this was now technically official Belasko spy business.

'All these babies, well . . . they just seem like normal babies,' suggested Alice, her cherry-red army boots squeaking along the floor.

They passed a room where a mother had just been presented with her newborn. The dad was taking a picture and wiping away a tear. Elliot made notes as they went.

'I know we all got freaked out by that baby in the square,'

said Venk, considering exactly what they were doing. 'But maybe we overreacted? I mean, maybe we got it into our heads that they were weird?'

'They *were* weird,' said Hamish. 'There was all sorts of stuff going on. Doors being sabotaged. Wallets stolen. And what about the ones pretending to be a man last night?'

'Well,' said Venk. 'I mean, I don't want to be funny, but . . . only you saw them, Hamish. Are you sure you weren't dreaming?'

Hamish knew what he'd seen. And his friends really wanted to believe him, but it was as if everyone's confidence had been knocked by the newspaper article. It had made them feel a bit silly.

'It's possible those babies in the square weren't growling,' said Buster. 'Maybe they were . . . grizzling?'

'Plus, it was quite windy last night,' added Clover. 'Perhaps *that* explains the runaway pram?'

'It wasn't runaway,' said Alice, firmly. 'It was being steered. Controlled. We all saw it avoid that poop.'

Hamish was grateful for Alice's support. But the truth was, even Hamish had started to doubt himself a little. He suddenly felt really embarrassed.

He'd dragged his friends all the way to Frinkley, and for what? Nothing had actually happened. What if was all in their imagination? And maybe Boffo hadn't deliberately been sick all over him for such a long time. Perhaps he'd just had some bad sushi?

What if it was time to admit Hamish simply didn't have any evidence?

They arrived at Boffo's old room and peered through the slightly open door.

Another baby was sitting in there, smiling and gurgling, as

his mum gently slept.

'Hmm. Well, they don't seem very scary right *now*,' said Alice.

Hamish glanced at Alice. Was she losing faith too?

He needed proof of what he'd seen. Some evidence that strange things were happening so they could get permission from Belasko to stop it.

Hamish spotted a CCTV camera above him and had something of a brainwave.

'The camcras!' he said. 'They'll have recorded the things I saw that day – and who knows what else!'

Suddenly the group found its energy again. They had a lead!

'That way,' said Alice, spotting the wires leading to a room marked **CONTROL**. 'Let's go!'

But, as they raced down the corridor in search of evidence, they had no idea that behind that door they would find much more than that.

11

Snipe

The **PDF** leapt into action the second they watched the security guard leave the control room to do her rounds. It was a shame no one had brought any action music with them, because this would have been the perfect time for it.

Venk flattened himself against the wall, holding his sunglasses at an angle so he could check round corners and make sure no one was coming. This was the best Venk could do at short notice. He sometimes worried he didn't have a proper place in the team. The others all seemed to have special skills and could leap instantly into action, while Venk just held their coats or made sure everyone stayed hydrated. He watched, slightly jealously, as Buster expertly whipped out his enormous key ring and started trying out all his skeleton keys on the lock of the control room.

Clover delved into her bag and pulled out a blue jumper, a beard and a home-made badge, so she could stand guard

100

outside the door and if anyone asked just point at her badge and say, 'I'm Jeff, the new security guard.'

JEFF THE NEW SECURITY GUARD

Elliot always carried a secret, hidden **PDF** memory stick in his sock, just in case he suddenly needed to download some important information from somewhere. He leaned down and took it out.

Actually, on reflection, maybe action music would have been overdoing it a bit.

'We're in!' said Buster, unclicking the lock.

Clover – sorry, *Jeff* – ushered everyone in, then slammed the door behind them.

Inside this dark room was a desk and about twenty television screens, each one flickering blue and showing what was happening around Frinkley Hospital.

SCREEN 1 showed an old man having his ankles waxed.

SCREEN 2 was just a shot of a woman eating some celery.

SCREEN 3 was the nursery.

'Download everything you can from Screen 3,' said Hamish. 'And then go back to the afternoon Mum and I visited Boffo. See what you can find from the corridors.'

'What's that noise?' said Alice, as Elliot got to work.

'What noise?' said Hamish. He couldn't hear anything and wasn't in the mood to be distracted either. They weren't supposed to be in here. In Starkley, they could get away with things like this, but Frinkley was different. It felt like enemy territory.

He spotted a copy of the 𝕱𝖗𝖎𝖓𝖐𝖑𝖊𝖞 𝕾𝖙𝖆𝖗𝖋𝖎𝖘𝖍 on the security guard's desk. He picked it up and looked at it more closely.

The Frinkley Starfish
Proudly published by Charmless Media A.X.A.R.

Charmless Media? Well, that was about right. Hamish wondered what the **A.X.A.R.** stood for. Some people said it was the *Association of Xtra Alternative Reporting*. He found Horatia Snipe's page again and peered at the picture of them all running away from the baby. Didn't people understand? That baby had looked vicious!

Hamish never understood why some people wrote this kind of thing. Why say such nasty things about people they didn't even know? Some people even wrote horrible things about people they *did* know. It seemed so pointless, putting this meanness out into the air. And you had to be careful. If

you wrote something horrible, it could stay online forever. Hamish thought a good rule was: *If you wouldn't say it to someone's face, you shouldn't write it at all.*

But Horatia Snipe seemed to be someone who was happy to write anything about anybody, so long as it made her look good. The truth was it didn't. Secretly, it just made people feel a bit sorry for her, and want to avoid her. I mean, who'd invite Horatia Snipe around for dinner when she might write a scathing article about the evening? For example, once a lovely lady named Jennifer Sniggles invited Horatia to supper and guess what they say Horatia did in return? She brought scorecards with her and a little desk, then sat behind it and loudly gave marks out of ten for each course that Ms Sniggles served.

STARTER: The cheese was too hot and the toast was not cooked. **2 OUT OF 10!**

MAIN COURSE: I expect more than a small blue bowl of curried baked beans and a sausage! **1 OUT OF 10!**

DESSERT: I was thoroughly distracted by your constant weeping! It put me right off my treacle! **0 OUT OF 10!**

Poor Jennifer Sniggles never cooked again. Although, judging by her menu, that was probably a blessing . . .

The point is, Horatia Snipe was one of those really awful people who do nothing but put negativity out into the world. She was a right old negatron and she thought it made her powerful.

Hamish knew all this about her and yet her words still hurt. The **PDF** were being called ninnies, when all they were doing was trying to save the world. *Everybody's* world.

'HAMISH,' said Alice, disturbing Hamish's thoughts. 'There's that noise again!'

'I heard it that time too,' said Elliot, looking worried, as the files downloaded from the computer. 'It sounded like it came from over there!'

Hamish turned to see the security guard's small kitchenette. Just a little sink, a toaster, a kettle and a tall fridge.

BA-RUMP. BUMP BUMP. CLATTER.

'It's . . . it's coming from the fridge,' said Alice, wide-eyed.

Normally, a fridge might make a low humming noise or perhaps the odd click or rattle as it settled down for the night. But this was different.

BA-KLANG. BRUMP. TAK.

This was all bangs and bumps and bops and clangs. Hamish could hear bottles being knocked against each other inside, clinking hard.

And now look! The fridge was rocking from side to side!

Was there a cat in there? Chasing a mouse? Wrestling with cheese?

'We should open it,' said Hamish. 'Elliot, are you finished?'

'Done!' said Elliot, tucking the memory stick back into his sock.

'Wait, Hamish . . .' said Buster. 'Don't open it. What if it's . . . I don't know. A ghost?'

Alice frowned. 'A fridge ghost?' she said. Alice had never heard of fridge ghosts. Why would a ghost want to haunt a fridge? Are spirits particularly into chilled meats?

'I'm opening it,' said Hamish, bravely. 'Stand by!'

And he grabbed the handle and slowly pulled. As he did so, the fridge door **creaaaaked**, and cold air began to pour from the edges. Alice jumped as eggs and cans of pop and old junk food tumbled out and spattered and clattered on the floor.

Hamish nearly yelped as the door opened fully and he saw what was sitting on the middle shelf of the fridge.

An enormous baby had its back to the kids and its face in a bowl of custard!

The cold air wisped around the baby as it furiously slurped the custard, rattling bottles of ketchup and sending plates of butter crashing to the floor.

It looked like a little goblin!

And then, sensing his presence, the fridge baby turned to stare at Hamish, and Hamish couldn't believe what happened next.

It got onto all fours and its eyes seemed to glow red, like some kind of terrifying, possessed dog!

Slaver poured from its mouth and ran down the fridge as the kids started to scream.

'DROOOOOOOOOL!'

it suddenly roared.

12

Baby Mayhem!

'**I don't know about anyone else,**' said Elliot as they ran from the control room, '**but I'm getting pretty sick of being yelled at by babies.**'

Hamish was shaken and shocked and shocked and shaken. That had taken the behaviour of the bad babies to a whole new level.

I mean, a baby yelling is one thing. But a baby in a fridge screaming, '**DROOOOOOOOOL**'?

Not to mention the slaver!

Now it was *undeniable*.

Absolutely undeniable.

There was definitely something wrong with the babies of Starkley and Frinkley!

The **PDF** ran out of the hospital and jumped on their Vespas to race back to HQ. Hamish didn't even care if anyone took a photo of them running away this time. Send it to the Starfish! Put it on the front page! That baby had been *terrifying*!

And now, more than ever, Hamish knew it wasn't alone.

As he shot back towards Starkley on his **Howler**, he saw babies staring from the side of the road, babies in car seats glaring out from cars and even a baby sitting on a cow in a field.

A terrible thought occurred to Hamish as he made it to Garage 5. All the babies seemed to share a certain look on their faces.

What if they were . . . *connected*?

Rather than lots of random acts of weirdness, they might all be on the same side. Like an army. A baby army.

A barmy!

And, if they were a barmy, this really *was* an **INVASION**.

They say some twins can read each other's minds and feel each other's emotions. When one of them is sad, the other might feel that way too, even if they're miles away, having the time of their life on a bouncy castle or eating free peanuts. What if these babies had some kind of kooky connection? What if they were all on the same *wavelength*?

Hamish needed to tell **Belasko** the second he had

absolute proof and time was of the essence. Babies can roam free. They can get in everywhere. They could start to slowly take over both Starkley and Frinkley, and no one would see it coming.

No one except Hamish and his pals.

But at least they'd seen more evidence of the crazy behaviour. And what's more – they had it on video.

Inside Garage 5, once the whole team were back, they gathered round the computer.

'Elliot, we need to study the babies. Show me the video you got from the hospital,' said Hamish and Elliot brought it up on the screen.

CHAOS!

It was pure **CHAOS!**

It was blimmin' baby bonkers!

The **PDF** watched in stunned silence as Elliot played the footage. They studied it carefully, like they were zoologists researching a bizarre new type of animal.

The same pattern kept repeating itself.

First of all, babies would be asleep in their mother's arms or gurgling quietly in their cots. All would be still. And then suddenly and for no apparent reason – like an invisible alarm had been sounded—

INFANT MAYHEM!

Babies would leap to their feet and immediately start peeing in pot plants!

Or drag themselves down corridors at speed, setting off all the fire extinguishers!

Hamish watched as one little baby threw a ball at a man drinking a can of lime pop. He fell backwards off his chair and poured the whole drink over face, his feet flew over his head as he tumbled over and he kicked an old man on the bottom, who in turn waved his stick in the air in anger, knocking a lady's hat off, and, as she bent down to pick it up, the lady bopped her head on the door, which swung open and banged a man's hand, who spun round and accidentally pressed the button to open his umbrella, which knocked a butcher clean off his bike, and as the bike kept going on its own it hit a taxi, and the taxi sounded its horn which woke the baby's mother, but by the time she opened her eyes her son was back in his bed looking very innocent and she was none the wiser as to what had just happened.

(If you managed to read that whole sentence out loud in one go, I will give you £2.50 and a neckerchief next time I see you.)

Look! Now a nurse was running straight down

the corridor in a state of complete and utter panic.

HIS ARMS WERE FLAILING!

HIS HAIR WAS WILD!

HIS TOP WAS TORN!

And on his shoulders . . . was a baby.

A crazy-looking baby, gurning wildly.

The baby's little legs were wrapped round the nurse's neck
and it was using its tiny fists to pummel his head. The nurse
screamed and ran into a sideroom – just as an old woman in
a wheelchair hurtled down the hallway behind him!

'WAAAAAH!' the old lady yelled, waving her hands around madly.

She was out of control!

Her chair bumped and bounced from wheel to wheel. She was about a hundred years old and must have been doing forty or fifty miles an hour!

'WAAAAAAAAAAAAH!' she yelled again, her hands now gripping the armrests and her eyebrows rising up and down like crazed worms doing press-ups.

A sprinkle of nuts and bolts tinkled down on the hard floor behind her like cheap stardust.

KABLANG! She burst straight through a set of double doors into the outside world and all you could hear was skidding and shouts and car horns.

'There!' said Hamish, pointing at the screen, as a tiny girl with a baby blue spanner crawled away. 'I saw that baby when I went with my mum to visit Mrs Quip in the hospital! She has to be involved somehow!'

Elliot pressed fast forward on the footage, trying to find the day Hamish had visited the hospital.

'Look!' said Elliot. 'There you are, H!'

Hamish looked at the screen. He saw himself leaving Boffo's room with his mum. Everything was peaceful, quiet and calm.

The second he left the hospital, however, babies poured out of rooms left, right and centre. It looked like that film, **KINGDOM OF THE MONKEY MEN**. Some were beating their chests, some were swinging from door handles and others were throwing magazines around.

'It's a baby swarm!' yelled Venk, his eyebrows shooting up in such surprise they nearly left his head.

And then – just like that – it was calm.

'They stopped!' said Hamish.

The **PDF** watched as, on the screen, all the babies simply went back to sitting or crawling around like simpletons.

'So, all of a sudden, the babies go mad and then they just go back to normal,' said Alice. 'Why?'

'Something must be making them act this way,' said Elliot, tapping his chin.

'What do you mean?' asked Buster.

'I don't think it can be free will,' Elliot replied, ominously. 'The babies aren't acting out because they want to. Otherwise, it would happen all the time, randomly.' He

looked at his friends, very seriously. 'This, my friends, is *coordinated*. Someone – or some*thing* – is orchestrating this.'

Hamish started to feel uneasy. They needed advice from a more experienced **Belasko** operative. One with great knowledge of children's behaviour.

He knew just who to ask.

13

Sweet Child
o' Mine

Early the next morning, Jimmy burst into Hamish's room
and started doing star jumps.

He seemed very excited and I suppose that was the only
way to cope with it.

'Wake up?' he yelled. 'Hamish, wake up?'

'What is it?' asked Hamish, blearily.

'I've been published!' he shouted. 'My important poetry
has been published!'

He held up a copy of that morning's 𝔉rinkley 𝔖tarfish.

Mr Massive was on the front cover lifting up a dumb-bell
with his teeth.

'The love of my life, Felicity Gobb, just dropped it round?'
he yelled, delighted. Felicity had a part-time job at Shop
Till You Pop and got all the papers: the Starkley Post, the
𝔉rinkley 𝔖tarfish. Even the *Urp Burp*. 'She told me to look

at page nine?'

He opened the newspaper, ready to share his moment of triumph with his little brother. But then he stopped. His face fell.

Hamish got up and read over his shoulder. *Oh, no.*

𝔉𝔯𝔦𝔫𝔨𝔩𝔢𝔶 ∗ 𝔖𝔱𝔞𝔯𝔣𝔦𝔰𝔥

WORST POEM EVER WRITTEN FOUND IN STARKLEY!

Stop the presses! The worst poem EVER has been found, and it was written in – you guessed it! – Starkley!

It's by someone called Jimmy Ellerby (12) and it's called ONCE I WAS A BABY?, which is hardly unique, because once we were all babies! We don't want to publish the whole poem as it's SO AWFUL! But here is the last part for you to 'enjoy'!

> *But now I am my own man?*
> *With facial hair and suntan?*
> *And one day I'll be older?*
> *Like a really mouldy boulder?*

Hamish checked who'd written the article. It was Horatia Snipe. Of course. He looked up at his big brother. He had gone pale and shaky. Why had Horatia Snipe done this? Why had the Frinkley Starfish published it? How did they get hold of it?

'Why did they say I was twelve?!' yelled Jimmy. 'I'm fifteen!!'

It was all so . . . MEAN.

And why was Horatia Snipe being so horrible about Hamish and his family and friends in particular?

'I'm so sorry, Jimmy,' said Hamish. 'I think your poems are brilliant.'

But Jimmy didn't respond. He just quietly folded the newspaper, left it on Hamish's bed and then walked out of the room.

Hamish wanted to go after him.

But he had somewhere he needed to be.

For years, tiny Madame Erroneous Cous Cous had travelled the four corners of the globe, bringing fine sweets and fancy candies back to her International World of Treats.

The shelves inside glistened with the startlingly colourful

fruits of her adventures. The sugar danced in the air like dust.

Actually, was it sugar? Or was it Parisian Perfumed Pickle Powder, which she'd bought from a dog in a waistcoat by the Eiffel Tower?

There were Tunisian Tongue Tramplers and *Hardy Hungarian Humbugs*, which also worked terrifically well as moth repellents.

Every week, there was something new to try. Just this month, Madame Cous Cous had started 'Scotland Season', with **Dundee Drizzle Balls**, **FIRTH OF FORTH FUDGENUGGETS** and a half-sucked jellybean she'd found under a seesaw in Arbroath.

For years, everyone in Starkley had assumed that this small, cloud-haired woman was just a dedicated and enthusiastic shop owner, keen to explore the world and uncover the greatest sweets imaginable.

But that was only her cover story.

The sweets she brought back from her foreign travels were just to make people *think* she was doing that. In fact, she was going on secret special missions for top Earth defence agency, **Belasko.**

In Italy, she'd once wrestled with the Italian Prime Minister and told everybody it was because he'd wanted the last box of Italian **Candied Prawns**. In fact, it was because the Prime Minister was an alien imposter attempting to take control of the country!

In Mexico, she'd brought back Mexican MIRACLE MINTS (which were so awful it was a miracle if you finished one), but not before she'd abseiled down the side of the Mexico City Hilton so she could stop the beasts of B.E.A.S.T. from having their intergalactic diamond-smuggling meeting!

She'd fought bears in Russia, slapped a spider silly in Saigon, fallen off a building in Burma and landed on a cow in Coventry.

She was Madame Cous Cous: special agent and snack enthusiast.

And, right now, she was staring at ten-year-old Hamish Ellerby and polishing her spectacles.

'A crazy baby in a fridge?' she said, having just watched the video from the hospital.

'A crazy baby in a fridge,' echoed Hamish. 'And that's just one story. Something is happening, Madame Cous Cous. Something is controlling the babies. And it's getting worse. They've started intimidating me.'

'You're being intimidated by babies?' said Madame Cous Cous. But she didn't say this in a mocking way. She said it like she'd heard it all before. Like she'd been waiting to hear it again.

Her face darkened.

'Babies are the perfect weapons against adults,' she said. 'It's genius. If a baby goes crazy, an adult is the first person to defend it. They'll tell you she's just tired, or hungry, or windy. If they catch a baby stealing, they'll say he's not stealing, he's *playing*. If a baby is sick on you, you forgive her. If a baby pees on you, you laugh. If a baby draws a map and plans a robbery, she's not evil, she's *advanced*.'

'Or they've had too much sugar!' said Venk.

'Nothing wrong with sugar!' said Madame Cous Cous, rapping Venk's knuckles with her stick and then gobbling down a **Peruvian Polo**.

'But babies aren't in charge,' said Clover. 'Parents are.'

'You'd be surprised,' said Madame Cous Cous. 'If a baby is up all night, so is a grown-up. And, once a grown-up is worn down and weary, they'll do anything for a quiet life.'

She whipped out a map and placed it on the counter.

'Look, if a baby screams on one street,' she said, trailing her finger across the map, 'but *doesn't* scream on another, which street do you think the parent will walk down? If a baby screams on the way to the coffee shop, but not on the way to the Play Centre, where do you think the parents will take them?'

'The Play Centre . . .' said Elliot, horrified.

'If it wants to be, a baby is like a screaming satnav for parents,' said the old lady, 'cleverly guiding them wherever they want to be!'

Maybe it was his imagination, but at that moment Hamish was sure he could hear a slow, rising baby scream from outside.

'I need to give you a history lesson,' said Madame Cous Cous. 'Fetch your father's Holonow machine.'

Of course. The Holonow. Hamish knew exactly where his dad kept the Holonow and why she needed this amazing invention.

Madame Cous Cous tapped the end of her long wooden

stick. As she did so, a small phone antenna shot out of the top. She had some calls to make.

'Also!' she said, remembering. 'I need some DNA that I can look at through my microscope. A saliva sample, something like that.'

Venk nodded and immediately spat in his hand. He offered it to her.

'Not *your* saliva, you nitwit!' said Alice. 'A baby's!'

Venk blushed with embarrassment and quickly wiped his hand on his trousers. Why did he always do the wrong thing? He'd get things right someday. He knew he would.

'Get me Control,' said Madame Cous Cous into her stick, holding it to her ear as she wandered away.

Hardly anyone knew, but, at the touch of a button, the old lady could turn her sweet shop into Starkley International Science Laboratory. She could analyse the baby DNA to see if there was anything odd going on.

And Hamish knew precisely where he could get some.

ⱨ⯑

Outside, the **PDF** were excited. Just ten minutes earlier, they'd felt like whatever was happening was beyond their control and getting on top of them. Now they felt like they were taking the reins again.

And word had obviously spread that the kids were up to something.

'Oh my GOSH,' said Hamish, opening the door and looking out in shock.

Outside the sweet shop were . . . babies.

Dozens of them!

Babies in prams on street corners.

Babies in slings outside shops.

Babies sitting in small, plastic, ride-on cars. Babies in baby seats staring from slowly moving cars. A baby in a baby basket glaring from a bike.

Each and every one of them was staring straight at the PDF while their parents seemed oblivious.

Had those parents been guided here? Suddenly the screams Hamish thought he'd heard made sense.

'They walk among us!' said Elliot, amazed but also terrified. 'Well, sort of crawl.'

'It's like they're waiting for something,' said Hamish. 'A signal.' He was right. They reminded Hamish of a camping holiday he'd been on with his parents where he'd watched a sheepdog in a field, waiting for its master to whistle. It had stood there ready, alert and tense. These were some very tense babies.

'Buster,' whispered Hamish out of the side of his mouth. 'Get to my house. My dad's Holonow is in his study drawer.'

'I could do it,' suggested Venk, wondering why Hamish never sent him on lone missions, but Hamish didn't hear him.

'The rest of you,' said Hamish, 'start gathering more evidence of bizarre baby behaviour. I want to make sure this case is watertight if we're going to call in help! Alice, you come with me.'

Hamish recognised one of the bigger babies. It was Runt Sneer's little sister, Rhubarb. She curled her lip at them. She was carrying a dull metal rattle, and slowly and threateningly beating it into the palm of her hand.

A baby in a sling stole a pen from his dad's pocket, then scratched a moustache onto the face of the baby in the Beautiful Baby Competition poster.

Another stared at the gang from a pram on the road opposite. It sucked on its dummy, then spat it out onto the ground without taking its eyes off them.

Hamish noticed that this baby was wearing a wristwatch and remembered his school project.

'Fact one about babies,' he whispered. 'You never see one with a wristwatch.'

'Why would a baby need a watch?' asked Clover, as Elliot gasped loudly.

'It only needs to know the time,' said Hamish, working it out at the same time as his friend, 'if it has *plans*.'

14

Bonny Bouncing Baby

Hamish stood in the doorway, wiped the nervous sweat from his forehead and put on the special face he used for meeting other people's parents.

He called it his angel face. Pretty much every kid can do one. It's a special expression that seems to say, 'Oh, look at me! I'm a little angel who can do no wrong! Hello, Mummy! Hello, Daddy! Please can I have five pounds for that chocolate ice-cream chipmunk?'

Yeah, I know ALL YOUR TRICKS, you crafty little dungtickler. I hope your parents aren't reading this book to you or THEY'LL know the truth too!

Alice tried to copy Hamish's angel face, but it was no good. Her face was just naturally grumpy a lot of the time and it was simply something she'd had to embrace. She always looked like she knew you were thinking of stealing her

sandwiches and was just waiting for you to own up. Even the fiercest teachers at their school always felt like they'd done something wrong when in the presence of Alice Shepherd.

'Okay,' said Hamish, aware that time was of the essence. 'This is where he lives. Remember, we're just dropping by because we missed him.'

Hamish rang the doorbell as Alice shifted her backpack, and a moment later Mrs Quip opened the door. She had food all over her top and a Cheerio stuck to her face, but seemed completely oblivious to both things.

'Hamish!' she said. 'Have you come to babysit?!'

'Oh, hi, Mrs Quip! No, we were just passing—'

'YOU *HAVE* COME TO BABYSIT!' yelled Mrs Quip, clearly delighted, even though that is most definitely not what Hamish had said.

But Mrs Quip had already grabbed her jacket and whipped

it over her shoulders like a matador, sliding both arms in at once. It was very impressive.

'I'll be back in fifteen minutes!' she shouted, delighted. 'You'll be fine - he's very advanced!'

Then she ran down the garden path shouting,

'FREEEEEDOOOOM!'

Alice cast Hamish a glance. He shrugged.

They walked into the hallway.

WHOA.

There was porridge all up the walls. Every picture frame had been knocked and bumped. There were clothes everywhere and baby bibs on everything.

It was like a bomb had gone off. **A BABY BOMB!**

'Uh, Hamish,' said Alice, standing in the doorway to the living room, looking puzzled. 'How old is Boffo?'

'Like, a few weeks?' said Hamish, joining her.

'Are you sure? He's *massive*!'

Hamish and Alice stood in the doorway and stared at the scene before them.

On the other side of the room, in the doorway to the kitchen, an even-more-ginormous-than-normal Boffo

Quip sat, wedged into a baby bouncer. He still looked like a baby . . . just a *lot* bigger. I don't know how to describe different-sized babies, so let me put it this way. If the first time Hamish had seen Boffo it was like looking at a little chihuahua, now it was as if someone had let a Great Dane loose in the house.

He was also reading the newspaper and had a coffee on the go.

'Well, Mrs Quip was right,' said Alice. 'He does seem rather advanced for his age.'

She wasn't kidding. He was wearing slippers and studying the crossword.

'Also, who calls a baby "Boffo"?' said Alice. 'It sounds like a card game your grandma makes you play in a caravan when it's raining outside.'

On hearing his name, Boffo rustled his newspaper and put it down. He looked up at them and smiled, just as creepily as ever.

'So what's the plan?' whispered Alice. 'Wait for him to spit on you so we can grab his DNA? Or are you hoping for another mega-vomit?'

At this, Boffo took one more sip of his coffee, then set the cup to one side.

He rolled up his romper-suit sleeves and took a step backwards.

'Where are you going?' chuckled Hamish. Boffo was strapped into the bouncer with nowhere to go. Or so Hamish thought . . .

Boffo took another step backwards.

'Hey, stop,' said Hamish, as the elasticated ropes started to strain against the top of the door.

But Boffo took another step backwards.

And another!

'Boffo, no!' said Hamish. 'The whole thing will come crashing down!'

The rope was tense now. The little hooks that kept it stuck to the door frame were shaking and shifting.

And still Boffo stepped back.

'Stop!' said Hamish, suddenly realising what Boffo was up to. All he had to do was take his little feet off the ground, and that bouncer would fire him like a catapult!

'BOFFO!' yelled Hamish, as Boffo lifted both legs and—

VWOOOOOOSH!

Hamish pushed Alice out of the way as Boffo shot *straight towards Hamish* at a *hundred miles per hour*!

Hamish just managed to fling himself back in time.

The elastic stopped Boffo centimetres from Hamish – just long enough for him to slap Hamish round the face!

Then **VWOOOOOOSH** he pinged straight back again, through the door to the kitchen.

Hamish hardly had time to come to his senses, when—

VWOOOOOOSH!

Boffo whizzed *straight back* towards Hamish, and

SLAP-SLAP-SLAP!

Another three baby slaps to the face!

'OWWWW!' yelled Hamish, as Boffo zoomed away again.

Alice clambered to her feet. Even though this was definitely a terrible, awful thing to be happening to her best friend, she couldn't stop laughing. Especially because there was still lots of life in that elastic. Boffo started to whizz straight back towards Hamish, clenching his fist, ready to deliver a *proper baby punch*!

Instinctively, Hamish reached out, and—

'GOT YOU!' he yelled, triumphant. He'd caught Boffo!

Hamish held Boffo at arm's length, trying to avoid his still swinging fist. But goodness, this was one heavy baby. It was like holding one of his dad's bowling balls! And, what's more, the elastic was really pulling at Boffo now. It was straining as the hefty infant tried to hit poor Hamish Ellerby.

Hamish quickly came up with a plan. All he had to do was keep out of reach and wait until the baby got tired of trying to bop him and then gently put him back where he'd started.

But Boffo was furious to have been caught.

His clenched fists shook.

He went bright red.

His eyes started to water.

Drool began to pour from his mouth.

As he struggled and strained to bash Hamish, spit flew from his gob.

'Alice! Now!' cried Hamish, and, once she'd stopped laughing, Alice got a cotton bud out of her backpack and popped some Boffo-spit on it.

Boffo's rage only grew. He took a huge great gulp of air and . . .

'WAAAAAAAAAAAAAAH!'

It. Was. Deafening!

The whole room shook. The windowpanes rattled. The plaster in the ceiling cracked.

Hamish's ears were ringing and his arms trembled from the strain. But he couldn't let go, because, if he did, Boffo would go flying!

'Hamish Ellerby, what are you DOING to my darling Boffo?' yelled Mrs Quip,

suddenly reappearing. She had her hands on her hips and a furious look on her face. And who could blame her? To anyone who didn't know what just happened, it really looked as if Hamish was about to fire a crying baby from a catapult!

'It's not what it looks like!' yelled Hamish, his arms now really aching.

'Activate your angel face!' whispered Alice. Hamish tried but he just looked mad.

And then Boffo smiled and let off a poisonous baby bottom burp.

Oh, the *smell*!

Hamish couldn't hold on any longer! His fingers slipped and—

TWANG!
BOING! BOING!

Boffo boinged back and forth for ten whole minutes before anyone could catch him.

He was like a pinball, shooting this way and that and knocking over lamps in the living room and pots in the kitchen.

BOING!

CLATTER

BOING!

KA-SMASH!

Mrs Quip watched her son fly around as if she was at a tennis match. She shook her head and wheeled out a fresh tank of Formula One, ready for another feed to try and calm him down after his ordeal.

'That's the last time I'm asking you to babysit!' she said, surveying the growing disaster area, and Hamish tried to hide the fact that he was delighted.

'Let's go,' said Alice, nudging him and holding up her cotton bud. 'We got what we came for.'

They might have got what they came for.

But they were about to get much more than they *bargained* for.

Call the Infantry!

'He's certainly got a pair of lungs on him, that Boffo,' said Alice, making sure the spit sample was safely put away in her Tupperware sandwich box. 'I've never heard a baby scream that loudly!'

But Hamish wasn't listening. He was looking around.

Something had happened to Starkley in the time they'd been in Boffo's house.

It was like the weather outside had mirrored Boffo's bad mood. The sky had darkened and storm clouds hovered above them. But there was also something in the air.

Not something you could touch or see. Something you could sense.

A mood.

Unrest. Anger. Frustration.

Hamish shivered.

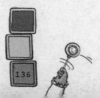

136

'Do you feel it too?' asked Alice.

And then from round a corner came a boy on a squeaky bike. He was screaming.

It was their friend, Grenville Bile!

He was huffing and puffing and ringing his little bell and going as fast as his legs could cycle. Unfortunately, because this was Grenville, that was very, very slowly indeed.

'Are you okay?' asked Hamish, walking alongside Grenville as he furiously pumped away at the pedals.

'What are you escaping from?' asked Alice, ambling along with them both.

'**B-b-b-b-b-b-BABIES!**' yelled Grenville, red-faced and out of breath. 'They've gone **NUTS!**'

Hamish and Alice stopped in their tracks and stared at each other. It had happened again. They had to get back to the sweet shop, pronto.

'Escape while you can!' yelled Grenville, now maybe four metres away. '**RUN!**'

И

The town square was abandoned.

Whatever had happened here had obviously happened quickly, unexpectedly and with great force.

There was rubbish everywhere. Crayon had been scribbled all over the doors. Cats hid in trees, too petrified to come down. Nubwick Stern, the piano teacher, who was known for never being confused or startled, wandered around, startled and confused. But no one else was anywhere to be seen. Poor old Starkley. This kind of thing was always happening!

Hamish could just make out what had once been Brenda,

Mr Longblather's 1984 Vauxhall Nova in terrier brown. The wheels had been unscrewed, the wing mirrors were gone and all four doors were missing.

Hamish stooped down to pick up something that had been left behind.

'A spanner,' he said, horrified. 'In *baby blue*!'

And then . . .

'Hamish! Alice!' yelled Madame Cous Cous, her hair all over the place as she flung open the door to her shop. **'Get in!'**

Inside, surrounded by the **PDF,** Madame Cous Cous seemed rattled but focused. She was in black **Belasko** overalls. Things were getting serious now.

She checked she had everything she needed, then walked over to a Billericay Bubble Gum machine and turned its little metal ratchet six times to the right, once to the left and twice to the right again.

A bronze ball of bubblegum bounced out.

Madame Cous Cous picked it up, took it over to her counter and placed it in a little hole.

Something clockwork inside the counter started to whirr, then the whole thing flipped over, revealing complicated scientific equipment. Rows of sweetie jars disappeared

from the shelves, replaced by petri dishes, Bunsen burners and samples pots. Madame Cous Cous flipped a couple of Cornish Cola Coins into her mouth and started to suck, for focus.

'Hamish, look at this,' said Elliot, holding up his camera. 'We had to run straight back in here when it happened, but look!'

He pressed **PLAY** and Hamish watched as, completely out of the blue, the babies of Starkley went absolutely crazy. It was just like the video from the hospital.

One second the babies were calm, sleepy and normal. Then, all at once, they began causing mayhem.

They tripped people up.

They smashed fire alarms.

They threw things, spat, blew raspberries and knocked cups from tables.

They grabbed at people's hair and pulled their dads' glasses off.

They chased people, and growled, and **ROARED**, and rammed their prams through doorways and into shops, knocking down displays and making everyone inside scream.

People tried to run for it, but these babies were FAST, pulling on shoelaces or kicking toy cars in front of them as they ran, so that grown-ups would slip over and end up in the bushes.

Some of the babies were on the bonnet of a little red car now, thumping away at it and pulling the windscreen wipers off. They were like deranged monkeys in a safari park!

'What caused that?' said Hamish, watching in awe. 'How could it happen?'

'Did you get the DNA?' Madame Cous Cous asked. Alice whipped off her backpack, found the cotton bud she'd kept safely in her sandwich box, flicked a few crumbs off it and handed it over.

Madame Cous Cous put the cotton bud in the analyser and began to run her tests.

Just then the ice-cream van – the **PDF'S** official vehicle – screamed up outside and out jumped Buster. The ice-cream van had had a bit of a makeover recently, because summer was nearly over and Buster's mum had decided that 'the state of the economy'

meant they couldn't just rely on selling ice creams. So now the van was also a mobile disco. Buster didn't really know what that meant, but he knew he loved disco balls. He'd stopped the car so sharply that the disco ball inside was now rocking back and forth like a yo-yo.

He cast a suspicious look up and down the street to make sure the coast was clear before running inside, carrying Hamish's dad's Holonow.

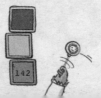

'What is happening now, children, has not happened for many hundreds of years,' said Madame Cous Cous, very seriously. 'Someone has harnessed an age-old technique for raising an army. **An army of CHAOS!'**

Hamish knew it. Hadn't he said this was just like an invasion?

'I don't understand,' said Venk, which wasn't an unusual thing for him to say. 'You mean the babies have formed an army?'

Madame Cous Cous fiddled with the DNA analyser. She reached over to a pot of sweets on her counter and pulled down a candy cane like a lever. Immediately, the analyser started bleeping and blooping. She stepped forward, took the Holonow from Buster and placed it on the floor in front of them.

'This will help to explain everything,' she said. 'Holonow – Code: Baby Fighters. Play.'

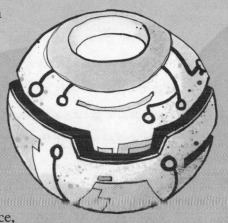

Immediately, the whole room began to flicker and change. The Holonow was a brilliant **Belasko** invention. It was a small device, no bigger than an orange, but when you pressed its button it put you right at the centre of an incredible hologram, showing you things you could never otherwise see. It could show you the surface of the moon as if you were standing on it. It could make you feel the past, as if you were travelling through time. Now, a thick grey fog began to roll through the shop and everything became much, much colder.

Hamish could feel sea spray in the air as it spattered on his face.

He could taste sea salt. The whole room seemed to rise and fall.

What was the Holonow showing them?

And then the fog cleared. Hamish and the **PDF** were right next to a GIANT VIKING LONGBOAT

as it sliced through choppy waters. They could see every detail close up: the huge planks of wood stuck together with rivets, and the heavy oars that rowed back and forth as the great ship powered towards the shore under a giant flag flapping loudly in the wind.

'WHOA!' yelled Buster, over the noise. **'VIKINGS!'**

'Exactly!' replied Madame Cous Cous, her hair puffing up the way it always did when sea salt got involved. 'But not the ones from the history books!'

Thunder cracked and lightning flashed as the longboat hit the shoreline, and a fearsome, high-pitched scream rang out. The scream of a hundred fearsome, fighting . . . BABIES!

Out of the boat they stormed, their hair in pigtails under little helmets, howling like wild beasts and waving their wooden axes.

'Ancient texts used to talk about "berserkers"!' yelled Madame Cous Cous. **'Fearsome Viking warriors that would howl like beasts and foam at the mouth! Also known as screaming and dribbling!'**

'Berserkers?' said Elliot. 'I take it that's where we get the word "berserk" from?'

'Yes,' said Madame Cous Cous. 'As in, "That baby has gone berserk!"'

'Wait,' said Alice. **'Warrior babies?'**

'It was said that the berserkers were so bonkers that they would gnaw the iron rim of their shields!' said Madame Cous Cous. 'Well, of course they did! They were teething!'

More and more yelling Viking babies poured from the boat, their faces daubed with colourful warpaint. They beat their chests as they splashed through the waves, crying 'Raaaargh' as they went.

Raaaargh!

'Naturally, historians have kept all this quiet,' Madame Cous Cous continued. '**Belasko** helped cover it up.'

'Why?' said Venk. 'Warrior babies sound cool!'

'The human race would come to an end if people realised! No one would ever have another baby if they knew that sometimes their baby's yells are war cries!' said Madame Cous Cous. 'Babies are highly emotional creatures. Baby uprisings have occurred all through time. But nowadays we bring our babies up *nicely*. We fill them full of milk and that keeps them sleepy and we play them lullabies and give them lives of luxury. We do everything for them. Modern babies aren't helpless: they're just lazy. It was very different in the past.'

She pressed the top of the Holonow and the fog, the water, the boat, the noise all disappeared.

Clover blinked a few times and wiped seawater from her face, stunned by what she'd seen.

'Of course, it wasn't just the Vikings and the berserkers,' said Madame Cous Cous. 'Many other cultures harnessed baby rage. Ninjas. Spartans. And it seems that's what's happening now: someone has found out about the collective power of babies. They're attempting to tap into them!'

'Tap into the babies?' said Hamish.

'Babies pick up on emotion,' explained Madame Cous

Cous. 'They can tell when someone around them is angry or stressed. And they have pure minds and hearts which means they can be influenced.'

Suddenly there was a **BEEP-BEEP-BEEP.**

'The DNA,' said Madame Cous Cous. 'It's ready.'

She waddled over to the analyser and gasped.

'The baby you got this DNA from,' she said, staring at the results, 'there's something deeply wrong with it.'

'What?' said Hamish, alarmed.

'The baby you got this DNA from,' said Madame Cous Cous, 'is *forty-two per cent tuna baguette*!'

She slapped her hand to her forehead in despair.

'Do you know what this means?' she yelled. 'We're up against an enemy that is nearly *half sandwich*!'

Alice blushed.

'Um, could that be because I kept the cotton bud in my sandwich box?' she suggested. 'I think you might have analysed my lunch. What happens if you ignore the tuna baguette bit?'

Madame Cous Cous rolled her eyes, then pressed a few buttons.

The screen began to flash red and black.

'Oh,' she said. 'Oh, dear.'

16

War Babies

'I don't believe it!' said Hamish, as the **PDF** sat huddled in the ice-cream van moments later.

If what Madame Cous Cous had told them was true – and it seemed to be! – then there was lots to do. They should call the Royal Air Force. And the Coastguard. And the Cub Scouts. And the Royal Society for the Protection of Everything.

Because if this was true – and I'll say it again: it seemed to be! – every street in Starkley and beyond had to be on high alert!

'Do we press the button?' asked Clover, referring to the last time Starkley had been under grave threat and needed everyone together.

'Not yet,' said Hamish. 'This requires kid gloves. Baby steps!'

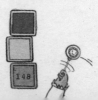

What Madame Cous Cous had revealed about Boffo's DNA was extraordinary.

'This baby contains an unearthly substance!' she had declared, pointing at the screen with her stick.

'That's why they wear nappies,' Buster had said. 'Babies contain *plenty* of unearthly substances!'

'No, no, far worse than that!' Madame Cous Cous replied, looking grave. 'I mean a substance which is literally not from this Earth.'

Well, that had stumped everybody. Particularly when Madame Cous Cous then revealed the baby contained something with the very scientific codename **F1**.

As they arrived at HQ, Elliot fired up the computer and started researching **F1**, while Hamish and Alice drew up a plan of action.

'Oh!' said Elliot, looking at a complicated diagram of compounds and scientific stuff and numbers.

'What?' said Venk.

'If this is true,' said Elliot (and don't forget I just said 'it seemed to be' *twice*!), 'it explains a lot about cows.'

'Absolutely,' said Venk. 'Hang on. What?'

'According to *That's Interesting!* magazine,' Elliot said, raising an eyebrow (which was actually the logo for *That's*

Interesting! magazine), 'when the first alien visitors came to Earth they were very drawn to cows.'

The kids all raised an eyebrow of their own.

Elliot spun his office chair around to face them, but he wasn't very good at that and ended up addressing a pot plant.

'Aliens would apparently often take a cow home with them across the galaxy. Cows became great status symbols. If you had a cow grazing in your cosmic field, you were quite the fancy person. For a while, early alien visitors would mistake cows for our leaders, because a lot of them thought they were more sensible.'

The **PDF** all stared at him. He was still talking about cows. And aliens. Had it all become too much for Elliot?

'Apparently, aliens were fascinated by a cow's milk. Its health benefits in particular. So they developed their own. A lot of it's produced on a planet called Screed.'

'And it's . . . *space milk*?' said Clover, astounded at the idea.

'Yes, kind of.' He stood and put his hands on his hips. 'They called it **F1**.'

Hamish looked shocked as a thought struck him.

'That's it!' he said. '**F1**. It's *Formula One*! That's what Boffo's on! That day in the hospital, Mrs Quip said she'd won a lifetime supply of it from the 𝔉𝔯𝔦𝔫𝔨𝔩𝔢𝔭 𝔖𝔱𝔞𝔯𝔣𝔦𝔰𝔥!'

Alice narrowed her eyes. 'She won it from that rag?' she said. 'Hmmm.'

'I don't know what the big deal is,' said Venk. 'Who cares where they get their baby formula? What are they up to, that's what I want to know!'

But Hamish had a more pressing question.

'Elliot, what exactly does **F1** *do*?'

How tall are you?

You're probably roughly child-sized, which is absolutely normal and natural – please don't worry.

But did you know that, in its first year, a baby grows a *crazy* amount?

Let's say you were – I dunno – about half a metre long when you were born. If you don't know how long half a metre is, it's about half the size of a metre-long baguette.

Anyway, if you *kept growing* at the *same rate* that you did in your *first year*, by the time you turned twenty, you'd be nearly eight metres tall.

That's the height of eight metre-long baguettes!

Or, to put it another way, the height of seven black cabs popped on top of each other!

That's far too big. You'd have to sticky-tape about twelve beds together just to get a good night's sleep.

But, according to *That's Interesting!* magazine, just adding a little Formula One to a baby's diet every day means that process speeds right up.

Formula One latches on to a baby's growth rate and *accelerates* it.

Which means that by the end of that first year of babyness, it's a *baby* that might be the size of two double-decker buses!

'Oh my gosh,' said Clover, when Elliot had finished explaining all this. 'Can you *imagine* the size of those nappies?'

Alice had heard enough.

'Boffo Quip!' said Alice. '*That's* why he's so massive! That's why he's got a better moustache than your brother, Hamish!'

But Hamish had a dark look on his face. Something had been bothering him ever since he'd watched the videos of the babies going crazy. What Hamish couldn't work out was why they'd turned at that specific moment. Everything had been fine one minute and then chaos a second after. So what happened *in* that moment of madness?

'Boffo's not just growing in size,' said Hamish, 'he's growing in influence.'

Alice stepped forward and nodded. She got what her friend was saying.

'He has the power to make other babies angry,' she said. 'Madame Cous Cous told us babies pick up on emotion.'

'The first time I met Boffo in hospital, he'd just had a meltdown. And I think it was during that meltdown that all the babies in Frinkley Hospital went mad,' Hamish said.

'And, when Boffo was at your house, he'd just had a tantrum, hadn't he?'

'Which was probably when the growling baby launched itself at us in the park,' Buster said, starting to understand.

'Wait, what about the crazy baby in the fridge?' asked Alice. 'Boffo was nowhere near that one when it shouted, "Drool!" and made its weird faces!'

'Maybe it's like a computer virus?' suggested Hamish. 'Once they're infected, any baby within earshot of another baby will pass it on. So, a baby's cry becomes a call to arms. Like shouting, **"Join me!"'**

'But join me to do what?' said Alice. There had to be more to it than this.

'I would recommend an immediate quarantine of the babies,' said Elliot.

'And we should remove any sharp implements from their

grasp!' said Clover.

'And ensure all cribs are secured!' said Buster. 'Luckily, it's past their bedtime. Most of them will already be in their cots, behind bars.'

Hamish nodded. Those all seemed very sensible ideas.

'And we should do a bunch of other stuff!' added Venk, trying to join in. Buster cast him a glance.

'Most importantly,' said Alice, 'we need to stop them from gathering in large numbers. That's where the real danger lies. Babies gathering in large numbers!'

Hamish nodded. And then gasped.

'**The Beautiful Baby Competition!**' he said, as beads of sweat began to prickle on his forehead. 'It's tomorrow! That's literally babies gathering in large numbers!'

17

Born to Run

The **PDF** were filled with a great sense of purpose, which is when they shone the most.

They knew something big and potentially very bad was going to happen. And they knew they had to stop it. Although one of the gang wasn't feeling quite as confident as the others.

Buster had noticed that Venk hadn't been his usual self since their escapade in the hospital. He took Venk aside to check that his friend was okay.

'I just feel that I'm not contributing as much as everyone else sometimes,' whispered Venk, a little sadly. 'I mean, you're great with tech. Clo is an amazing master of disguise. Elliot can translate basic Latin. I just feel like I don't have a speciality.'

'Well, maybe not having a speciality *is* your speciality,' suggested Buster. 'And don't worry. Not everyone is born

knowing immediately what they're best at. You'll find your moment, Venk. I'm sure of it.'

'Oof!' said Hamish, leading the gang out into the cold evening air. 'Do you feel that?'

The **PDF** clattered out of Garage 5 after him and stood still for a second.

'Bad vibes,' said Clover, adjusting her black **Belasko** boiler suit. 'The world feels . . . grumpy.'

'So what do we do?' said Alice. 'Get the baby competition cancelled? I mean, what do we say? You know what parents are like. They're panicky old oddballs!'

'Should we sound the alarm?' said Buster, because Starkley had a brand-new **Only in an Emergency!** siren these days, suitable only for the grimmest of threats. Hamish had to be very certain before doing that. The alarm was wired straight to Belasko and would be beamed to wherever Dad was right now. Their important work would be interrupted as they turned round and shot home.

Also, it was just past seven o'clock and all the grown-ups would be sitting in front of *Life's a Dream with*

Vapidia Sheen and you only interrupted that in a real crisis.

'Something's not right,' said Hamish, zipping up his suit. 'Something feels different.'

The town was deathly silent. There wasn't a trace of a hint of a rumour of a cousin of a noise. The gang stood and listened to absolutely nothing at all.

Moments later, trusting their instincts, the team was in the van.

'Let's do a drive-around before we panic,' said Hamish, and Buster put his indicator on and turned right into Myna Street.

All the way along the road, houses had their curtains open and their lights on. Hamish cupped his hands and pressed them up against the van window, between the pictures of ice creams and disco balls. He could see mums and dads, grandmothers and grandfathers, brothers and sisters, some of them surrounded by baby toys, sitting in front of the television with cups of tea and plates of biscuits balanced on their knees . . . every single one of them were fast asleep.

All down Elderberry Avenue, the flickering blue light of the TVs bounced off the cars outside. The noise of gentle snoring drifted through windows as the **PDF** spotted more

clapped-out, exhausted grown-ups dozing in front of the telly.

'Everyone's worn out,' said Hamish, almost to himself.

In some of the upstairs windows, the soft yellow of night lights cast a glow around dangling baby mobiles.

Everything seemed strangely peaceful. Weirdly normal.

Apart from one thing.

'Look up there,' said Clover, pointing at a window. 'That's odd.'

Hamish looked up. In the window of No. 22 Elderberry Avenue was the camera from a baby monitor. Now there's nothing unusual about that, is there?

Except that this camera was pointing outwards – towards the street.

Hamish frowned and stared up at No. 35 as they passed. That was the home of Mole Stunk. Her mum had just had a new baby. Everyone had wanted to know what was wrong with the old one. But she'd called it Millie (short for Millipede) and as they passed her house . . .

'The Stunks' camera is facing outwards too,' said Hamish.

It was the same at No. 18 Viola Road.

And 12 Knotweed Lane.

'I think we're being watched,' said Hamish in alarm, as

they trundled along. 'The babies are using the monitors to monitor us.'

'What was THAT?' screamed Buster, slamming on the brakes as something scuttled across the road.

The ice-cream van skidded to a halt on the high street. Disco records slid everywhere.

Outside Pizza Hat, under the colourful bunting that stretched this way and that, four metal bins rattled from side to side.

'Maybe it was a fox?' said Clover.

Buster moved off and the team strained to see if they could spot anything.

They circled round, past the town square, and as they approached Myna Lane . . .

CLABANG! CLATTER!

From the side door of No. 26, a cat flap rattled. It had swung open with real violence and slapped back down into place.

'Did anyone else see that?' said Hamish.

He was sure something had burst out of the cat flap. Something heavy. It was too dark to see exactly what. And now it had padded away into the undergrowth of the garden.

As the PDF watched, a whole tree started to sway as something brushed past its trunk and moved through the bushes of the garden next door at great speed. And with it came a noise almost like a drumbeat.

Chakkachakka.
Chakkachakka.
Chakkachakka.

Wait – that wasn't a drumbeat.

That was . . .

'A *rattle*?' said Alice.

'Let's get out,' said Hamish. 'We should follow it on foot! Keep a low profile!'

Buster pressed a button and the back doors shot open. Hamish, Alice, Elliot and Clover leapt out.

'You and Venk get back to base,' said Hamish. 'Make sure whatever's in the bushes sees you go so it thinks we've left!'

Buster winked at him and turned the radio right up. He honked his horn and drove off at speed, disco music blaring from the windows.

The bushes moved slightly until the van was out of sight, then began to stir again.

Hamish and the gang kept low and moved fast, following the noise and watching as something in the dark stalked through gardens and over fences.

It was moving with great determination. It obviously had somewhere to be.

At the corner by the Snooze Agents, as the kids jogged behind it, it suddenly leapt from the bushes and continued to run in the street. Now it was lit by the street lamps, and Hamish could not believe what he was seeing.

A small, powerful, muscular baby. Pounding down the street like a crazed escaped monkey. Clover couldn't help but gasp.

The **chakkachakkas** slowed and the baby stopped in its tracks. It caught its breath, panting and growling. Steam rose from its body.

It turned and stared at them.

18

Bye, Baby Bunting!

The baby stared at Hamish, Alice, Elliot and Clover as its heavy pants fogged the air.

Er, hang on.

I mean the baby was panting heavily.

I don't mean it was wearing heavy pants and they were somehow fogging up the air.

You might wear pants like that but this baby didn't.

'This is one of those moments,' said Hamish, stretching his arms out protectively in front of his team, 'where either *it* chases us or *we* chase *it*.'

And then **POW!**

The baby turned and began to pound away, scuttling on all fours quickly through the town square and past the old clock. It leapt over a bin, knocking tin cans from the pile and sending them noisily bouncing off the pavement.

'Looks like *we're* chasing *it*!' yelled Hamish and the four friends set off in hot pursuit.

Alice took the lead. She was still Starkley Under-12s 100-metre champion, after all. But even she had to admit it felt weird chasing a baby.

Around the corner the tiny beast ran, its little feet and hands slapping against the concrete. It was faster than a kid on a bike!

But the **PDF** were hot on its heels as they skidded round the corner and . . .

'Where's it gone?!' Alice said.

They stood in confusion at the end of the high street, staring out at the closed shops and abandoned street in front of them.

The baby had disappeared into thin air.

What? How? Where had it gone?

Was it some kind of magical shapeshifter?

Had it transported itself to another realm?

Could it move through time and space?

Or had it just scrambled up a drainpipe?

'Look!' yelled Clover, pointing upwards.

The baby had scrambled up a drainpipe! And was about to do something insane.

It stretched one foot out and tapped the Union Jack bunting that criss-crossed the street above the shops.

'No, baby weirdo!' yelled Hamish. **'Don't do it, baby weirdo!'**

But the baby weirdo looked determined. It was going to walk the bunting like a tightrope!

Hamish and the others fanned out, standing right beneath it in case it fell.

It put one chubby foot out . . . and the bunting began to sway.

To the right it wobbled!

Then to the left!

The kids gasped!

The baby put its arms out for balance, before putting its other foot on the line.

What was it doing? Bunting was no place for a baby!

'Babies can be so *childish!*' said Elliot, furious.

Now the baby was wobbling back and forth, teetering over them, spinning its arms as it tried to keep its balance. It was terrifying. The kids all stayed right underneath, just in case. Somehow they'd gone from enemies to potential saviours in the blink of an eye!

And then, getting used to the rope, the baby started to walk . . .

Faster . . .
And faster . . .

And then it started to *RUN* down the bunting, **LEAPING** from one set to the next, **ZIGZAGGING** across the street as the **PDF** chased underneath.

'It's too fast!' said Alice, keeping her elbows and knees high.

Off the baby ran, scampering up another drainpipe and standing on a rooftop, silhouetted by the full moon, then leaping into a tree with a star jump.

But Hamish and the gang weren't giving up that easily. As it slid down the trunk and continued to run, they ran harder, chasing the fleeing baby as it pelted out of the town and away into the fields.

'I think it's heading to Frinkley!' said Alice, slowing her run. '*Hasta la vista*, baby!'

The others huffed and puffed and came to a standstill behind her. Elliot had a stitch and Hamish was all muddy.

Which is when the noise began, stopping Alice in her tracks.

A **juddering, thuddering, gear-shifting roar** of a noise.

'What's that?' said Clover, feeling small in this big field by the road.

Suddenly the kids were lit up by strong and powerful headlights. They quickly ducked out of sight.

The four of them watched as the first in a long line of huge, thundering, sixteen-wheeler lorries turned down the road.

The scream of the engines was immense. The smell of diesel filled the air. They were coming in off the motorway and indicating left for Frinkley. The field blinked orange.

One enormous, ginormous, super-mega-normous lorry after another.

167

'Are they petrol tankers?' asked Alice.

But Hamish shook his head, pointing at the words written on the side of the huge silver tanks in dirty red letters.

'There's enough there to feed every baby in Britain,' whispered Hamish.

And as the tankers rolled on towards Frinkley, and the noise began to fade, a lesser team than the **PDF** might have been so frightened and distracted by the sights they'd seen that they could have missed hearing Starkley's **Only in an Emergency!** siren cut through the brisk night air.

Buster and Venk must have run into trouble!

19

Go, Hamish!

It wasn't just the long, rising wail of the siren that told Hamish that Starkley was in trouble.

Buster and Venk had activated the town's Emergency Response System too. Every street light in Starkley was now quickly flashing red and blue, lighting up the sky. Whole banks of clouds above the town turned red and blue in quick succession.

'Well, I don't think anybody's asleep any more,' said Alice, as they paused for a few seconds before breaking into a run.

'What can the matter be?' wondered Elliot, leaping over a puddle.

'I'm still worried about those tankers,' said Hamish, casting a glance behind him. 'Where were they heading? The same place as that baby, I'll bet.'

As they got closer to the edge of town, there were more flashing lights. But these were from a police car. PC Saxon

Wix was barking orders at his colleagues, telling them to put police tape up and start dusting the area for fingerprints.

Concerned residents were huddling in doorways, whispering and muttering among themselves and nervously shaking their heads. There seemed to be panic in the air.

Madame Cous Cous stood outside her shop, talking into her stick, pacing up and down and shaking her head.

Hamish and the gang ran straight to her, but she waved them away, mouthing, '**Belasko** – no time.'

She was on the phone to **Belasko** again? That meant Hamish and the gang could expect a call soon too.

'Well, at least we know the emergency alarm works!' said Clover.

Over by the town clock, other grown-ups like Mr Longblather and Frau Fussbundler pinned **Belasko** badges to their lapels and wore very serious looks on their faces indeed. Hamish saw Buster and Venk chatting animatedly to Mr Slackjaw about what they'd seen. Venk was doing an impression of the way the baby had run. It wasn't bad but he'd never win *Starkley's Got Talent* with it.

'Clo, Elliot. Go and tell Mr Longblather about the lorries,' said Hamish. 'Then meet us back at HQ. I'm going to head back with Alice – my dad will probably call us soon.'

Hamish and Alice knew they needed clues. They dashed to the computer in Garage 5 and found the *Frinkley Starfish* website. Hamish's tummy flipped when he saw the main story.

THE PDF? STARKLEY'S BIGGEST JOKE!
by Horatia Snipe

Can I ask you a question?

Who are these stinky Starkley children who keep insisting they've saved the world?

The PDF – what does that even stand for? Perfectly Dim Fibbers?

Anyone can see they're exaggerating!

First it was so-called 'WorldStoppers' they claimed to have vanquished!

WorldStoppers? Starkley is the one place you don't have to stop the world!

It's already stuck in time!

I bet if it had an airport, the captain landing a plane would say, 'Welcome to Starkley – where the local time is 1983!'

Then there were 'the Terribles' – harmless-looking monsters who I think stole my nickname for Starkley schoolchildren. They're the real 'terribles'!

Then there was the time their whole town was overrun by 'Venus spytraps'.

Oh, really? Looked like a lot of old weeds to me. And what does it mean if you get woods? Poor town hygiene!

Let's face it – this bunch of kids may have 'witnesses' and 'evidence' of their 'heroics', but I need more than 'facts'. And my gut feeling is it's all nonsense!

These kids should stay in Starkley where they belong, instead of coming over here to Frinkley where they might poison the minds of our glorious, pure-minded children as they run away from tiny, gentle babies! Is it any wonder crime's been up lately?

Down with the PDF!

And underneath, in the comments section, lots of people who seemed to be from Frinkley had written their replies.

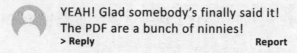

YEAH! Glad somebody's finally said it! The PDF are a bunch of ninnies!
> **Reply**   **Report**

Good on ya, Harrashya, you tells it like it is.
> **Reply**   **Report**

The PDF pretend they is fighting monsters. Well said, comrade!
> **Reply**   **Report**

'What's wrong?' said Alice.

'Nothing,' said Hamish. 'Just people thinking they're clever by being mean.'

Hamish saw that there was even a button on the website that said

CLICK HERE TO COMPLAIN DIRECTLY TO STARKLEY TOWN COUNCIL.

That would go straight to his mum. No wonder she'd been inundated lately.

Hamish clicked the page away and found the Search bar.

He typed in *babies*.

A few headlines came up.

RECORD YEAR FOR BABY BIRTHS IN FRINKLEY

was the first.

Then he typed in *crime*.

Oddly, crime had gone up in Frinkley at around the same time that they started having more babies. But they were weird, inexplicable crimes, like mysterious, unsolved burglaries where there was no sign of how anyone got in or out. Some people had started to blame each other in the comments under the articles. Neighbours now looked at one another with an unwelcome suspicion, or blamed 'outsiders', like people from Starkley.

A thought struck Hamish. He typed in *burglary* and *cats*.

'What on earth are you doing, H?' said Alice. 'This is not the time for hilarious cat videos.'

But Hamish smiled. His detective work might just be paying off. From the stories that started appearing, it seemed that almost everyone who'd been burgled had something in common.

There was a picture of a woman named Granny Pog. She was looking sad and pointing at where her old table lamp used to be before it was nicked. And she was *holding a cat* . . .

Then there was Dimmock Peaknuckle. His favourite book, *The History of Felt*, had been stolen. He'd only turned his back for a minute. He'd had to *feed his cat* . . .

'What do you think it means?' said Alice, confused when Hamish pointed them out to her. 'That there are . . . *cat* burglars?'

'No,' replied Hamish. 'I'm saying that everyone who was burgled had a cat. Which means there's a very good chance that everyone who was burgled . . . had a cat flap.'

Alice remembered what they'd seen earlier that night and realised what Hamish was trying to say.

'Baby burglars?!'

Was this why the police were in Starkley tonight? Was that why Buster had sounded the **Only in an Emergency!** siren? Had they all seen a baby burglar escaping the scene of the crime tonight?

'Hey, look at that,' said Alice.

At the bottom of the page, in a tiny story almost hidden away, was the headline:

OLD PETROL STATION BEING REDEVELOPED BY FRINKLEY NEWSPAPER GIANT

'GUYS!' yelled Clover, suddenly bursting into HQ, closely followed by the others.

'What happened?' said Alice. 'Buster, why the alarm?'

'Was it the baby?' said Hamish. 'Did they find out a baby had disappeared?'

Clover took a step forward.

'It's all the babies, H,' she said, her face now pale and scared. '*All the babies* have gone!'

Eyes on
the Prize

'This is bad, H,' said Hamish's dad, pacing up and down the room with his arms folded.

At least, he appeared to be in the room. The gang had fired up the Holonow when the call had come in, meaning it was as if Agent Angus Ellerby was actually there.

'How many babies are we talking about?' asked his hologram.

'All of them,' said Hamish. 'And I suspect something similar might have happened in Frinkley.'

'Frinkley?' said Dad. 'Why Frinkley?'

Hamish explained his thoughts. He told his dad exactly what had been happening from the start.

The strange babies in Frinkley Hospital.

The fact that all the babies born there seemed a little ... unusual.

The one they'd just chased through the fields outside Frinkley.

The curious case of massive Boffo and his strange DNA.

Their suspicions about his growing influence on other babies.

The recent rise in burglaries. The baby monitors facing the street.

Hamish's dad listened intently, but, when Hamish mentioned the strange petrol tankers carrying Formula One, he clicked his fingers and looked alarmed.

'Formula One?' Dad said. 'How much Formula One?'

'Lorries of it,' said Alice. 'Litres and litres and litres.'

'Baby advancement formula,' he replied. 'Speeds up the

development process. Give babies enough of it and they'll be doing crosswords by the time they're two weeks old!'

Hamish's dad suddenly seemed to be talking to someone they couldn't see. He made furious gestures and mouthed things like *Code Grey* and *Return Ship Now*.

'Kids,' he said, turning back to them. 'I think we may be heading for a **BABY BOOM**.'

'A Baby Boom?' they all said at once.

'Yes. A cataclysmic event. A once-in-a-generation moment. A point of no return. One in which the babies rise up against us. If these babies can communicate their rage to each other, and if they're big enough to attack, just imagine what they could achieve!'

Hamish thought about it. What his dad was describing sounded like Baby Mayhem. *Bayhem!*

It would be like the Viking invasion they'd seen on the Holonow, but in real life! Or hordes of marauding Spartans! Ninjas on every corner!

It was all becoming clear. Boffo had been chosen by some evil higher power to become some kind of King Baby – he could certainly influence the others. And if they were full of Formula One . . .

PDF were suddenly under. 'I'll be there as fast as I can!'

'How long?' said Hamish, relieved. 'Where are you?'

'I'm about a hundred and sixty-three thousand miles away,' he said.

'Is that in another county?' asked Venk, stunned. 'Are you anywhere near Milton Keynes? My uncle Anil could give you a lift back.'

Dad pressed a button on his watch. The whole room filled with stars and planets and galaxies.

'I'm at a space hotel called the Andromeda Star. I've been looking out for Scarmarsh,' he said. 'But it seems he knew I was coming. He's in hiding. I haven't been able to find him anywhere.'

Hamish and Alice swapped glances.

'What do you mean?' said Hamish.

'He's in hiding?'

'Well, all my information has led me to a dead end.'

Hamish's mind was racing. Could it be that Dad was mistaken? Scarmarsh had tricked them all before – why couldn't he be tricking them now?

What if Scarmarsh had fooled Dad?

Got him out of the way?

Sent him 163 thousand miles away on some wild goose chase?

Leaving Starkley vulnerable to a **BABY BOOM!**

'Dad,' said Hamish, with a sinking stomach. 'On your trip to find Scarmarsh, did you pass a planet called Screed?'

'Yes,' said Dad. 'He'd been spotted there, but then we were told he'd pushed on further so we gave chase. How do you know about Screed?'

And then Dad's eyes widened, turning from shock, to realisation, to anger.

'*Screed!*' he said, finally putting it all together. 'There's a huge **F1** plant there!'

'It's Scarmarsh, Dad!' said Hamish. 'He must have gone to Screed, but doubled back and paid people to give you bad information!'

Scarmarsh with the glare . . .

Scarmarsh with the Starkley obsession . . .

Scarmarsh who Hamish knew would never be far away . . .

'I'll be back as fast as I can, H,' Dad said, getting out his Andromeda Starpoints loyalty card and signalling to

someone that he needed to pay his room-service bill and pronto. 'A few days. Do what you must. Get to Madame Cous Cous. I'll call her now and fill her in. She'll be able to help you until I get back.'

As the **PDF** jogged to the International World of Treats, Hamish came up with a battle plan.

'We need to go to Frinkley,' he said to his friends. 'We have to find out where those tankers were going.'

Where would petrol tankers even be going at this time of night?

Wait.

'What was that in the paper about a petrol station?' said Hamish.

'Just that the newspaper people had bought it?' said Alice, before realising something. 'That's a very weird combination of businesses, isn't it? Why would a newspaper buy a petrol station? That's like starting a shop that sells books about railways and combining it with gentlemen's haircuts.'

'Might I remind you that our official vehicle is both an ice-cream van and a mobile disco,' said Buster. 'So I'm not sure we're ones to judge. Talking of which, I have a few modifications to make . . .'

'I'll come with you so I can start researching petrol stations,' said Elliot, which was a first.

'Wait for me,' said Clover. 'I'll pack a few disguises!'

The team was pulling together once again.

'Time for Cous Cous,' said Hamish, which was both accurate and also sounded like the name of a really terrible recipe book.

Madame Cous Cous looked deadly serious when they walked in. There was no time for small talk any more than there was time to make an origami pelican or wallpaper a church. So Hamish launched straight into it.

'I was under the impression Axel Scarmarsh worked for the Superiors?' he said. 'I thought the Superiors were like . . . well, his superiors?'

'They were,' replied Madame Cous Cous, folding her stick in two. 'But they lost interest in Earth when we sent them packing the last time. It was too much like hard work! I've been talking to some of my contacts and it seems Scarmarsh has done a deal with the Superiors. He agreed to forever leave Part A of the galaxy alone in return for Part B.'

'Part A and Part B?'

'A is the "Awesome" part. The Superiors took Nebulous,

Imperia, the tropical twin planets of Thrust, plus Go-Getta and Ultra-500.'

'And what about B?' said Hamish.

'B,' she said. 'Aka the "Bobbins" part.'

'Hang on,' said Hamish, looking a little offended, if I'm honest. '*Earth* is in the *Bobbins* part? The bad part?!'

Madame Cous Cous nodded.

'Scarmarsh was given Earth, Burf, Mundania, Klaxon, Polyfill, Harrumph and Turd.'

Hamish clenched his fist.

He hated Scarmarsh, ever since the day Scarmarsh had tricked him into breaking into his evil lair at the top of the Post Office Tower in London. Scarmarsh was always one step ahead. And, if he had indeed parted ways with the Superiors, he'd be free to do whatever he liked. Hamish knew Scarmarsh loved Earth and was fixated on Starkley.

That always seemed strange to Hamish. If Scarmarsh wanted, he could strike anywhere in the world. Bogota. Berlin. Burton-on-Trent. Yet he was choosing the one place he knew was packed with **Belasko** operatives and where he'd met resistance before. He was choosing the very place **Belasko Agent of the Year**, Angus Ellerby, called home.

There must be a reason for this obsession, thought Hamish.

And Hamish was right. Handing the Superiors the more attractive part of the galaxy was just a cunning part of Scarmarsh's plan. He'd been studying their weaknesses, and one day he knew he would overthrow his weird lizard masters (he already had a few ideas how). But, for now, he just needed them out of the way – along with **Belasko** – and distracted by what they thought was the main prize.

Of course, the Superiors had no idea about the truth behind Scarmarsh's actions. But now, in this sweet shop, Hamish was starting to work things out. And he was getting closer to the truth . . .

'I think that quite often,' he said, softly, 'the most dangerous person in the world is not the person who's in charge. It's the one who's second-in-charge.'

'How come?' asked Alice.

'Because you're not looking at them,' said Hamish. 'And they're quietly biding their time before they strike.'

Madame Cous Cous nodded, wisely.

Then, just as all that slotted into place for Alice and her friends, the whole town shook as an almighty **BOOM!** rocked the skies . . .

Where When How What Why?!?

In the skies over Starkley, it was like someone had unleashed a zillion fireworks.

A streak of fire hung in the air, a bright orange against the ink-black of the cosmos.

'What was THAT?' yelled Venk, utterly startled.

After the **BOOM** had come a **ROAR**.

The screech of metal came after that, as something huge and hulking spun and twisted in the air, disappearing past the trees before anyone could see what it was.

The gang ran outside and stared up at the sky.

'Something *big* just entered the atmosphere,' said Elliot, adjusting his glasses. 'And I'd say it was headed towards Frinkley.'

'Good!' said Buster. 'We always get the trouble. Monsters, aliens, massive snapping plants. Let Frinkley deal with something for once!'

But Hamish knew better. 'Scarmarsh,' he said, darkly.

The gang began to panic but Hamish needed to focus. Dad was 163 thousand miles away, and space traffic at this time of night was terrible. This was up to Hamish. And things were starting to make sense.

If Scarmarsh was here, it was because of the babies.

Find the babies, find Scarmarsh.

Find Scarmarsh, stop the **BABY BOOM**.

'This isn't a time for panic!' said Hamish, clapping his hands together, then pointing importantly in the air. 'This is a time for action!'

As the ice-cream van tore down a country lane, the fire in the sky had all but disappeared. It had left a smell in the air like the one you get after a particularly enormous intergalactic bonfire. And, as the **PDF** arrived in Frinkley, they found much the same scene as they had left in Starkley.

Confused parents wandering around, holding hands and comforting each other.

Police cars and flashing lights and people searching bushes and outbuildings.

Houses with their doors wide open and their lights on and blaring tellies.

People staring upwards and pointing out where they'd seen the fire in the sky.

Posters saying, *Beautiful Baby Competition: Postponed Until Further Notice!*

A few people glanced suspiciously at the **PDF'S** van as it whispered through town. Hamish knew the people on street corners and staring from the pavements were probably saying mean things about them. Maybe they thought the **PDF** had made all this happen so they could step in and pretend to save the day, just like the *Starfish* was always saying they were doing.

There had obviously been a baby break-out here in Frinkley

too. Babies running for the hills as their parents dozed on sofas. Babies leaping over fences, crawling under bushes or diving through cat flaps. They even heard people talking about one baby who had apparently escaped by riding a dog. Hamish would bet his last Chomp that they'd all headed to the same place, as if guided. But the baby exodus had happened before the fire had raced through the sky to announce Scarmarsh's arrival.

So *who* had guided them?

'Hamish! Have you seen Boffo?' came a panicked voice from somewhere to the left of him.

Buster stopped the van. It was Mrs Quip. She had run straight up to them, obviously too upset to care what other people in Frinkley thought about the **PDF.**

'Will you help me find my tiny, delicate angel?' she pleaded.

'Of course,' said Hamish. 'That's why we're here.'

A few more people glanced at the **PDF** now, with perhaps a little hope on their faces.

Alice noticed someone hanging around by the bushes. A tallish woman with short hair who looked scared about approaching. And then she found the courage to step forward, into the light. She was carrying a pad and pen, which she suddenly put away.

They all recognised her immediately.

It was Horatia Snipe.

'You!' said Alice.

'Can you help us?' asked Horatia.

'I'm Hamish Ellerby. You made fun of my brother,' said Hamish. 'That was mean.'

'I'm so sorry,' said Horatia. 'The new owners made me do it. They don't want us to write nice stuff about you. People love it! I've lost count of the number of readers who've sent me letters telling me they hope I'm offered a new contract and re-sign! Look!'

She pulled out a letter from her pocket and Alice read it.

'That doesn't say re-sign,' said Alice. 'That says *resign*!'

'The bosses say it's much more interesting if we're mean,' said Horatia.

'Interesting for *nitwits*!' said Buster.

A few Frinkley people looked at their shoes, a bit ashamed.

'The owners never come into the office,' said Horatia. 'We just get emails telling us what to do and if we don't we get the chop.'

'Well, these new owners need to get a grip,' said Alice. 'Who are they anyway?'

'Charmless Media,' said Horatia. 'They've been buying up everything in Frinkley. *Sharm!* Cars. Larch Molar's Bags.

They've even blocked the radio signals so that everyone here can only get their news from one place.'

'Let me guess,' said Hamish, sarcastically. 'The 𝔉𝔯𝔦𝔫𝔨𝔩𝔢𝔶 𝔖𝔱𝔞𝔯𝔣𝔦𝔰𝔥.'

'Who's your boss?' demanded Alice.

'I've never met her,' said Horatia. 'None of us have.'

'What's her name?' asked Elliot, from the back of the van.

'Mrs Salt Chard,' said Horatia. 'All anyone knows is her name and that her registered business address is offshore.'

'Offshore?' said Alice.

'Well, specifically a boat,' said Horatia. 'HMS *Carras*. That's all I know.'

HMS *Carras*? Something about that rang a bell with Hamish. Some distant, hidden memory he couldn't quite put his finger on.

Elliot pressed a piece of paper into Hamish's hand.

'Anagrams,' he whispered.

S ~~O~~ R
A A ~~S~~
~~M~~ H

Sharm! Cars – Scarmarsh

Larch Molar's Bags – Scarmarsh Global

Charmless Media A.X.A.R. – Axel Scarmarsh Media

Mrs Salt Chard – Scarmarsh Ltd.

HMS Carras – Scarmarsh

Hamish nodded and folded the paper.

'So can you help us?' asked Horatia. 'Can you help Frinkley?'

Hamish just didn't know if he could trust Horatia Snipe, who he still suspected to be a fully paid-up member of the *Association of Xtra Alternative Reporting*. What if she was in touch with Scarmarsh? What if she was part of the trick? She could be lying about not knowing who she worked for . . .

Alice, however, had no such reservations.

'You have a choice to make now, Snipe. Help the side of good or help the side of evil. Tell us where the old petrol station is, then take a permanent break from making fun of people.'

She put her hands on her hips. 'What's it to be?'

Horatia thought about it, then clambered into the van.

'I think I know the place you mean.'

Babes in
the Woods

Horatia Snipe plonked herself down in the passenger seat of the ice-cream van and Hamish eyed her suspiciously.

In many ways, this woman was the enemy. The number of mean things she'd said about Starkley was breathtaking.

She also couldn't stop dropping in bits of information about Frinkley, like they were on some kind of guided tour.

'To your left is the new potato-recycling centre,' she told them, 'where more than three hundred potatoes are recycled every day!'

'What do they turn them into?' asked Venk.

'Just into potatoes again,' shrugged Horatia.

Snidey Ms Snipe didn't seem so bad in real life. It was like if she had to look you in the eye, rather than hide behind what she said on the internet or in the paper, she had to be nicer. She gave Buster the directions to the old, abandoned

petrol station in the woods.

'Why would there be a petrol station in the woods?' asked Buster.

'Well, that's why it's abandoned,' said Horatia. 'It's not like the squirrels needed any diesel. Bad planning really. No, it's very quiet. No one ever goes there.'

'You once said Frinkley was better than Starkley in every possible way,' said Hamish, quietly, trying to see if she could be trusted. 'You said Frinkley gave the world Mr Massive and if it was Starkley it would've been Pedro Puny.'

'I did,' said Horatia, her face falling. 'Sometimes people do or say things they don't want to when they're struggling. I got myself into a mess where everybody expected me to be mean all the time. That's why they'd read my articles. And I was afraid that, if I didn't keep going, people would stop reading. Then Mrs Chard sent me a message to say I'd better keep going because it was good for the paper.'

'There's something I have to tell you about "Mrs Salt Chard",' said Hamish, deciding to take a chance on Horatia. 'But in fact I think it might be better if I just showed you.'

'Park here,' said Horatia, as the van slowed under a dark canopy of trees as black as tar. 'The petrol station is just past those bushes.'

The group crept through the woods from the little country road – trying to stay out of sight – and the first thing they noticed was the noise.

A growing hubbub.

The sound of machinery.

The low growl of engines.

Something was pumping. It sounded the way Hamish imagined an oil field to sound: all winches and pistons and pumps and hydraulics.

'It's just down this way,' said Horatia. 'I have to say, this is very exciting. I feel like a proper investigative journalist!'

Everyone was being careful not to step on any broken branches or fallen logs so as to be as quiet as possible. But the ground underfoot was dark and soft and covered in old pine needles.

Clover, who had her camouflage kit out in the van, had given everyone a 'woodland' helmet to wear, featuring pine cones, sticks and fake beetles. 'All that noise! This petrol station doesn't sound very abandoned to me.'

There were tree branches and leaves all over the road alongside them. Hamish looked up. Whatever had come down this road recently had been tall enough to knock into the trees.

'The lorries,' he said. 'They must have come this way.'

'Shhh,' said Horatia. 'I think whatever you're looking for is up ahead.'

They dropped to their knees and started to crawl through the bushes on their elbows. A badger thundered past from nowhere. Foxes darted away. Something was really disturbing the wildlife.

'Do you smell that?' said Alice, sniffing the air.

It was the bonfire smell. Except now it didn't just smell of fire. It smelled of fuel.

'Petrol?' said Alice.

'No,' said Hamish. 'That smells different to this . . .'

He'd last smelled something similar when he'd been in London. At the very moment Scarmarsh blasted off into space.

They crawled further and then, bending away the thick branches of a bush . . .

'Oh my gosh,' said Horatia Snipe. 'The babies!'

They had found them. So. Many. Babies.

But they seemed different.

'What's happened to them!?' said Horatia. 'They're like wild animals!'

Hamish's mind raced. It was as if the babies were involved in some weird tribal ritual. Some of them danced around in their nappies. Others slapped their chests and whooped. Some wore torches on their foreheads and spun around, as the lorries continued their chug-chug-chug noises in preparation for who knows what.

And there, in the middle of it all, strode a fearsome, giant figure.

'Who's that man?' said Horatia.

'That man,' replied Hamish, 'is a baby.'

Boffo!

Horatia looked like she wanted to faint. She stared at Boffo, still holding his Toppy Sparkles in one hand and some kind of spear in the other, and shook her head. He really was massive.

'That must have been a difficult birth,' she said, all pale. 'I pity the poor mother.'

Boffo slapped other babies on the back with glee, sending a couple of three-month-olds flying. The Starkley and Frinkley infants were gathered round several of the lorries, in front of the strange old garage, and unrest was in the air.

'I think they're hungry,' said Venk.

Sure enough, a moment later, Boffo started to pound his

chest like a gorilla, then reached up to press a huge red button on the back of the first lorry.

The babies cheered as the tanker started to judder. A hose at the back began to buck wildly and rise and fall like a big red snake. Boffo picked it up and released the nozzle at the end, and the hose began spraying Formula One high up into the air. It rained down on the babies, who danced in it, opening up their baby gobs and guzzling it as it fell.

The second and third lorries did the same thing, as Hamish and the gang stared in horror from the bushes, the stench of cinnamon hitting their faces like they'd walked into a wall of it.

'It's like some kind of Baby Fuelling Point!' said Alice, horrified.

Horatia clapped her hand to her forehead. 'This is the story of the century!'

Other older babies lunked out from the petrol station. They had biceps and were the size of sumo wrestlers. One baby girl now had a full beard and what looked like a tattoo of an anchor on her arm.

This sailor baby grunted at Boffo, then picked up a nozzle from one of the petrol pumps. She started to spray Formula One into the air, its thick cinnamon aroma mixing with the smell of Scarmarsh's rocket fuel until Hamish's nose started to tingle.

Actually, talking of Scarmarsh, where was he?

And that was when – **KASHUNK!** – the floodlights came on.

Gigantic, enormous white floodlights.

The **PDF** hadn't been able to see it in the dark, and they'd been too distracted by frolicking babies to take it in, but right behind the petrol station was a huge, glazed structure. It had different levels, each of them round. And there were long metal poles at the top. Hamish immediately knew what was at the bottom.

Rocket boosters.

It was the top of the Post Office Tower! The one that used to be in London, before it was stolen by . . .

'ATTENTION, BABIES!' Axel Scarmarsh boomed as he strode through the automatic doors of the Post Office Tower.

He seemed somehow taller than the last time Hamish had seen him.

He wore a black cape.

A black, well-cut suit.

A golden medal on a red ribbon.

'Feed! Feed yourselves stupid!'

he shouted. '**GORGE YOURSELVES** on this *special edition* Formula One! The finest and most nourishing of all the formulas!'

Behind Scarmarsh stood two of his awful henchmen, the Terribles, dressed like midwives. They slathered and slickered, their terrible tongues trailing from their terrible mouths. One of them picked up a baby and cradled it, drool and slather pouring out and coating the poor infant's head.

Scarmarsh laughed as he watched the babies spraying the hosepipes hither and thither.

'Does your mother's milk do for you what Formula One can?' he said, staring down at Boffo and the sailor baby and another one whose nappy seemed to be made out of a giant British flag. 'The mothers of Frinkley certainly seem to believe what they read in the papers! How simple the adult mind is! How easy to change people's habits in just a few weeks! They were all too keen to fill their babies with this vitamin-boosted milk!'

The babies around him seemed almost to grow by the second, like they were filling with pride.

'You have followed all my orders. You have mirrored the emotions of the Chosen One!'

Boffo grinned, pleased with himself, and hugged Toppy

Sparkles tighter.

'And now your parents are exhausted, weakened, docile,' said Scarmarsh, and Hamish noticed that Horatia was writing all this down as fast as she could. 'For too long now, I have tried to create my own armies, when all along I could simply have influenced one!'

Hamish's mind was in overdrive.

Of course – it all made sense.

Scarmarsh had grown weary of creating monsters like the Terribles, or building robots like Hypnobots, or breeding plants like Venus spytraps. It was all so time-consuming. But babies were already here on Earth. If he could control the babies of the world, he could tire out the grown-ups. Wear down their resistance. He could make the babies wake thirty times a night if he wanted. Then cry and scream all day long. He could turn adults into exhausted zombies, unable to fight back because they hadn't slept in weeks.

That explained why all the parents in the town square that day hadn't noticed their babies' weird behaviour! And why they were all asleep in front of their tellies by seven o'clock each night!

But what were Scarmarsh's plans for the babies?

If he could link their emotions with Formula One and use

Boffo as an amplifier, he could take their pure minds and make them do whatever he liked. He could send them into museums to rob all the artwork! He could send them into battles, like a fearsome Viking horde! He could make them test out cat flaps for reputable cat-flap companies keen on cheap market research!

Babies didn't yet know the difference between good and evil. So all Scarmarsh had to do was feed them up on Formula One and control their emotions.

Using Boffo Quip.

But how was he controlling Boffo?

That was the bit Hamish didn't quite understand yet. Hamish felt sure that, if he could work that out, he could stop all this.

Was Boffo radio-controlled? Had he been hypnotised?

'Tomorrow comes the **BABY BOOM!**' yelled Scarmarsh, as a Terrible in a mechanic's outfit tinkered with the lorries beside him. 'Be READY. Gather together for what will be **ANARCHY!**'

Hamish and the **PDF** all took sharp breaths.

'Now **RETURN TO YOUR HOMES AND YOUR CLUELESS, STINKING PARENTS AND PREPARE!**' screamed

Scarmarsh, turning and disappearing back into the tower, flanked by his beastly Terribles.

And Hamish Ellerby and his friends dived for cover, as suddenly hundreds of terrifying, heavy-set babies thundered through the woods towards them, heading for home.

Abra-kebabra

'So let me get this straight,' said Horatia, bumping around in the ice-cream van, checking her notes. 'The Formula One connects the babies?'

'Yes,' said Alice, hanging onto the sides of her seat as the **PDF** tore away from the woods. 'And it makes them bigger. Stronger. And magnifies their emotions. An angry baby will be even angrier if it's had Formula One.'

Horatia shook her head, amazed.

'And if the chief baby is angry enough?' she said.

'It looks like Boffo is the Chosen One,' said Hamish. 'The others will "catch" his emotions. Babies can sense feelings.'

'Why Boffo?' asked Horatia.

'He's the most advanced, because he's been on Formula One the longest,' said Hamish. 'He probably has to shave. What if Scarmarsh chose him because my mum has been spending so much time with Mrs Quip? What if it was a way of getting close to us? But *why?*'

He looked out of the window. Even though they were going at about forty miles per hour, he could see babies in the field next to them keeping up! Some leapt over fences; others pounded away on all fours with their tongues trailing out of their mouths.

'What's the link between your mum and Scarmarsh?' said Horatia, writing everything down, grateful for such a scoop.

'My dad has . . . a particular set of skills,' said Hamish, not wanting to mention **Belasko** and the fact that his dad had just checked out of a space hotel. After all, Hamish had taken the Starkley Oath. 'Scarmarsh is always trying to get at Dad. I think choosing Boffo was just another way of getting close to him. He knew my mum was good friends with Mrs Quip. It was a clever way of sneaking a spy into our house. No one ever suspects a baby of espionage.'

'This is the strangest story I've ever worked on,' said Horatia, pleased that, for once, she wasn't just saying everything was terrible.

As Buster's van skidded to a halt in Frinkley to drop off Horatia, the police were still out and about, comforting concerned parents and older siblings.

'Look!' yelled a police officer. **'The babies!'**

Looking sweet and innocent and as if butter wouldn't melt in their mouths, dozens of tiny, smiling babies started slowly crawling over the road towards Frinkley.

Not running, not bounding on all fours, just crawling, the way babies do. Even the newborns – fortified by Formula One – were managing it.

The whole town erupted in cheers.

'They're back!' shouted a mum, running over to pick her baby girl up in her arms. 'Oh, thank goodness! Where have you been?! Oh, my darling Nutella!'

More and more babies crawled through hedges, giggling and gurgling sweetly, not for one second making anyone think they'd been running with high knees through fields a moment before.

Nor would anyone ever have guessed that they'd been gorging themselves on **Formula One** from petrol tankers deep in the woods while an intergalactic bad guy and his monster sidekicks cackled and rubbed their hands with glee.

I mean, sure, all the parents desperately barked questions at their infants, like, 'Where on earth have you been?!' Or, 'When did *you* start crawling?!' But all the babies did in return was put on their angel faces and gurgle sweetly – and you know how much grown-ups love an angel face.

And, yes, of course, many of the parents quietly wondered why their babies seemed to weigh more than a bowling ball all of a sudden – but maybe that just meant they were healthy?

But really all anyone wanted to do was welcome their very advanced and clever darling babies back with open arms, put them to bed, make sure the cat flaps were locked and go straight back to sleep.

'The rest of the babies will be arriving back in Starkley soon too,' said Alice, darkly. 'Ready for the **BABY BOOM**.'

'Thanks for your help in finding them,' Hamish said, turning to Horatia. She smiled, pleased to have done something good for a change. 'If you want a story . . .'

He hesitated. Should he really be telling her this? But she had proved herself to be trusted, hadn't she? He made a decision.

'If you want a story then come to the **Beautiful Baby Competition** tomorrow in Starkley town square,' he said.

'I'm supposed to be there anyway for the paper. Is that where you think the Baby Boom will be?'

Hamish nodded.

'Something's going to happen,' he said. 'They'll all be gathered together and if enough babies get angry and magnify their emotions, they'll be heard by babies for miles around. Babies all over the region will join them. Then babies all over the country. We're talking about a baby-pocalypse. We need to keep our eye on Boffo and watch out for Scarmarsh.'

Hamish was trying to look brave and like he knew what he was doing. The truth was he wasn't sure that even the PDF could stop Scarmarsh this time. There'd be no relying on help from Dad. Hamish had to deal with Scarmarsh on his own.

Well, that wasn't true. He had his friends. And they'd coped before.

'The problem with babies is they're unpredictable,' said Alice, wisely. 'Who knows what's going on inside their heads most of the time? Sometimes you'll pick one up and he'll just blow a raspberry in your face. We need to read up on them – get inside their minds. Find out what makes them tick.'

All this sounded great, but she had no idea how she was going to do it.

And just then – just as their old enemy, Horatia Snipe, was

about to walk away – her eyes lit up like a baby's novelty nightlight.

'I think I know who can help,' she said.

ᚼᚻ

Ten minutes later, the **PDF** were outside a dark and empty shop on Frinkley high street. It was a takeaway. They rang the doorbell for what must have been the tenth time.

'Kebabaret!?' said Alice, looking up at the sign, which was of a woman doing a high kick next to a kebab pole. 'Why did no one tell me you could get kebabs in Frinkley?'

'It's fairly new,' said Horatia. 'I'm ashamed to say I gave it a terrible review in the 𝔉𝔯𝔦𝔫𝔨𝔩𝔢𝔶 𝔖𝔱𝔞𝔯𝔣𝔦𝔰𝔥. I didn't even try one of the kebabs. I think that may have affected business.'

Alice rolled her eyes at her and pressed the doorbell again.

'Isn't it a bit late for food?' asked Venk, and Buster kicked him in the shin as if to say, *Don't ruin this for me!*

The upstairs window squealed open. 'Who is it?' yelled a woman in curlers.

'Nurse Pickernose!' said Horatia. 'My name is Horatia Snipe and—'

Immediately, Nurse Pickernose started throwing whatever she could at Horatia. Fruit. Old jam jars. A chicken shish kebab.

'**HORROR-ATIA SNIPE!**' she yelled. 'What was it you said in the newspaper about my kebabs? Oh, yes. **"CHICKEN SHISH? MORE LIKE CHICKEN SHEEEEESH!"** Oh, but you gave my *rivals* a *great* write-up!'

'Really Fried Chicken and Discount Kebabs are owned by my bosses!' cried Horatia. 'I'm sorry!'

'You even got **MR ELBOWS TO GIVE ME THE ELBOW!**' screamed Nurse Pickernose.

Clover shook her head, disapprovingly.

'That guy Elbows is an absolute dingbat,' said Alice, as the good nurse took her slippers off and lobbed them straight at Horatia's noggin.

'Wait!' pleaded Horatia, her hands in the air. 'Please, listen! It's a matter of life and death! We need your advice!'

'My advice?' said Pickernose. 'My advice on *what*?'

'Babies!' said a desperate Hamish. 'There's a problem with the babies and only you can help!'

Nurse Pickernose's face softened.

Babies.

The one word that meant more to her than 'kebabs'.

The one thing she missed more than anything.

Her little Frinkley wrinklies.

But no. She had turned her back on that way of life once and for all!

'I DON'T WANT TO TALK ABOUT BABIES! NOT SINCE THEY ALL WENT MAD THAT NIGHT AND PEED ON ME! IT WAS LIKE A CO-ORDINATED ATTACK, I TELL YOU!'

She put her hand on the window frame, ready to shut it again.

'Please, Nurse Pickernose,' tried Hamish. 'Once a nurse, always a nurse. And if the world needs a nurse's expertise, isn't it a nurse's sworn duty to give it?'

Alice nudged Hamish, impressed. That was a good line.

Nurse Pickernose looked uncertain. Hamish had struck a chord with her. Now he just needed to seal the deal.

'*Activate your angel faces!*' whispered Hamish, and the **PDF** beamed as many delightful, innocent smiles at her as possible.

'I'M COMING DOWN TO LET YOU IN! WHO WANTS CHIPS?'

24

Midwife Crisis!

The kids learned a lot from Nurse Pickernose in just seconds.

Mainly how not to decorate a room.

It seemed Nurse Pickernose had really thrown herself into the world of fast food since things hadn't worked out with the peeing babies.

She had chicken-tikka-masala-coloured wallpaper. She had a bed shaped like a bag of chips. She had a sleeping bag that looked like a pitta bread. (You had to slide in one side and then zip yourself up.) She had pillows that looked like pickled onions, a rug that looked like a slice of processed meat, pyjamas with peas all over them and chicken nugget slippers.

Nurse Pickernose also taught them that their plan wasn't half as clever as they'd hoped it was.

'No, no, no, no, no!' she said, when Elliot had explained what they'd come up with so far. 'Babies just won't go for

that kind of thing! You have to get into the mindset of a baby if you're to conquer one!'

And so she'd sat them down on some baked beanbags and helped them draw up a battle plan.

'You'll need soft toys. Songs. Snoozes,' she said.

I'll be honest – it didn't sound like much of a battle plan.

But Hamish's dad always said you had to know your enemies. You had to understand how they think. Well, that's very difficult when your enemies are babies. Who knows how those oddballs think? It's not like you can gain much psychological insight just by looking at them. Even if you could read their minds, you'd struggle to work out what they were up to.

A typical enemy-baby's thought process might be:

MUST DESTROY!

Oh, look, a fly. Yes. I was right, I am currently wetting myself.

DESTROY! DESTROY!

Oh, look, a fly. I think I'm going to wet myself.

I can make noises. Blippy-blappy-bloo.

MUST DESTROY THE GROWN-UPS' WAY OF LIFE!

Hey, why am I so wet?

It's very difficult to know quite what a baby's big plan is, just as it's difficult to know what a bird's favourite hat is or what the moles on your arm dream about when you go to sleep.

Of course, some people never grow out of those kind of random thoughts, and go on to live rich and rewarding lives, usually either as teachers or presidents. But, when you have a pack of these miniature lunatics all banding together and acting as one, well, it can spell danger.

'This explains a lot!' Pickernose said. 'I'd thought all my babies had finally turned on me that awful day in the nursery! But they hadn't. They were simply picking up on the emotions and actions of one baby in particular! Boffo Quip!'

Using nothing more than a kebab wrapped in tinfoil, she trained the **PDF** in the rudimentary arts of baby whispering. Each of them took turns holding the kebab and whispering reassuring things to it. Now they had a better idea of what they had to do when a baby was upset, when they might be about to throw a tantrum, when one needed more chilli sauce – that kind of thing.

As the gang prepared to leave her flat, Hamish turned to Nurse Pickernose.

'Will you help us?' he asked. 'It's not really our area of

expertise. And don't babies require . . . specialists?'

Nurse Pickernose smiled.

'My days of dealing with babies are over,' she said, before her eyes turned misty. She cast a sad look at her medical skateboard, now under a glass dome on a plinth in her room, never to be ridden again. 'That day in the nursery, I made two promises to myself. One: *Never go back*. And two: *Always carry a moist towelette in case someone pees on you.*'

※

The next morning, at 8 a.m., the first thing the gang noticed as they sat up in their beds was the smell that now seemed to hang over Starkley.

As Alice drew back the lightning-bolt curtains in her room in Viola Road, it was like a low dark cloud was draped across the other houses around town.

'Cinnamon,' she said, sniffing the air.

And then she pulled on her combat shorts, laced up her army boots, checked the blue streak in her hair and slid down the bannister to her front door.

'Can you pick up some eggs on your way home, love?' called her mum, but Alice was already on her scooter halfway down the path, sailing towards Hamish's house to collect her friend.

As her hair flapped behind her, she wove round bollards and bounced off pavements, whooshing and scraping the ground as she rounded the corners.

Everywhere she looked, doting parents were pushing prams towards the square for the competition.

People carriers and *Sharm!* cars were dropping off excited families, who'd made their babies look as shiny and lovely as possible. Not one of these parents seemed ready to admit that something weird had happened to their babies in the night. Not one of them seemed ready to admit that their babies had got a lot . . . well . . . *bigger*.

Dads had babies strapped to their chests as usual – but the babies were now almost as big as they were, their hairy legs bopping against their father's, and their enormous feet trailing along on the ground.

Some babies were literally wedged into car seats, and needed the help of the taxi drivers to pull them out.

Others walked alongside their bigger brothers and sisters, wearing their mum's dungarees and towering over their siblings.

Of course, all the parents thought this was fabulous.

'It's the organic carrots we buy,' said a lady being dragged past by her baby. 'They may be pricier but you can see the benefits!'

This had been another stroke of genius on the part of Scarmarsh. Parents only want to see the best in their children.

Take you, for example.

You and I both know that there has never really been a stinkier, grubbier child than you.

You and I both know that you smell of moss and bits of old bark.

But your mum? Your dad? They think you're epic.

You and I both know that you spend most of your time thinking about cakes or what's on telly.

But your parents? They think you're a genius, sent to save the world!

You and I both know that when you dance you look like a weird fish gasping for air.

Your parents? They think you're a rare talent with a unique and original dance style.

So these dingbat Starkley parents – and the dingbats coming in from Frinkley – simply thought their babies had had an extra growth spurt. One that made them special. They decided their ear-blistering temper tantrums were merely the frustrated cries of an artistic genius. That the fact that they were now big enough to wear their dad's shirts was a compliment to their father somehow.

It's exactly why the angel-face trick works so well. Grown-ups *want* to believe the best of children.

The smell of cinnamon grew more intense as Alice whizzed past the town clock, where already the **Beautiful Baby Competition** banner had gone up and the seating had been arranged.

At 9 a.m., all manner of babies would sit on those chairs,

and those chairs would then collapse under their weight and have to be replaced by special, reinforced chairs.

The point was, Alice decided, if she and Hamish didn't do something fast, the **BABY BOOM** would begin.

25

Baby,
Get Back

When Alice arrived at Hamish's house at 8.15 a.m, she was in a state of real panic.

'These are **BIG** babies!' she said, rushing straight to his window and watching a mother struggling to push a buggy while a ginormous infant sat bolt upright, eating a leg of lamb. 'I don't know what else Scarmarsh put in that Formula One at the petrol station, but let's just say these babies are some healthy-looking meatballs!'

Hamish was exhausted. He'd been up most of the night, trying to work out what Scarmarsh's next move would be.

If all the giant babies were guided by Boffo, then Hamish needed to know how Scarmarsh controlled him.

He'd made a list, as Hamish likes to do.

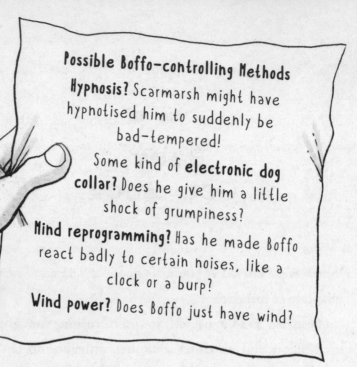

Possible Boffo-controlling Methods

Hypnosis? Scarmarsh might have hypnotised him to suddenly be bad-tempered!

Some kind of **electronic dog collar?** Does he give him a little shock of grumpiness?

Mind reprogramming? Has he made Boffo react badly to certain noises, like a clock or a burp?

Wind power? Does Boffo just have wind?

None of it seemed quite right.

But somehow, at some point, Scarmarsh would have to give a signal. And that signal would trigger Boffo, which would trigger all the other babies. The cries and screams of all of the babies at the competition would be the start of the **BABY BOOM**.

Hamish didn't like to imagine what might happen next.

If the **BABY BOOM** was strong enough, other babies would hear it – maybe babies in Peppermill, Urp or Thackeridge – and they'd join in

Then their **BABY BOOM** would be picked up by

babies in nearby shopping centres, nurseries or crèches, and the noise would multiply and spread like a baby computer virus – until eventually, some weeks later, babies in Bogota and infants in Iceland and tots in Tottenham and newborns in New York would all join the cause!

And rise up against the grown-ups.

Last night, Hamish had seen a small glimpse of that kind of chaos, and it was not something he wanted to happen on a global scale.

The question was: how could they stop it?

'So how do we stop it?' said Alice, clapping her hands together, certain that her friend would have a plan. But Hamish didn't.

'We should call the others,' he said, picking up his walkie-talkie. 'PDF HQ, are you there?'

He thought Clover, Buster and the others would have been up late too, wracking their brains.

But no one responded.

He pressed the **CALL** button again.

'**PDF** HQ, this is Hamish, come in.'

He listened but all he could hear was static.

'All the radios are still on the blink!' said Elliot, shaking his head, when Alice and Hamish had arrived at Garage 5 after rushing there in a tizzy.

Clover, Elliot and Venk were already there, but their walkie-talkies weren't working.

Hamish remembered what Horatia Snipe had said about the radio stations disappearing. Scarmarsh was making sure that everyone got their news from one place – the 𝔉rinkley 𝔖tarfish – which meant he could control public opinion. But that was dangerous, wasn't it? Because anybody could write anything, couldn't they? Like that the PDF were running away from babies, when of course they'd been running away from *demon* babies. Of course, if you miss out the word 'demon', it's a completely different story!

Scarmarsh's genius had been to take what the people of Frinkley had and use it against them.

He had taken their suspicion of Starkley – and used it against them.

He had taken their paper – and used it against them.

He had taken their babies – and used them against them.

But that didn't explain why the walkie-talkies didn't work . . . But the radio stations vanishing might be a clue?

'Maybe that's how he controls Boffo?' Hamish said. 'Could Scarmarsh be using radio waves somehow?'

'Hmm,' said Clover. 'Boffo doesn't strike me as a radio-controlled baby. I didn't even know you could buy them.'

'Okay!' said Buster, striding into the room and interrupting their conversation. 'I've made a few modifications to the van. We should be ready for anything, no matter what this Baby Boom is.'

'How did you get on, Clo?' asked Alice.

'Oh, I think you'll be very happy with what I came up with,' said Clover. 'Though of course I'll need a volunteer.'

A volunteer? For one of Clover's plans?

Everybody immediately looked at Venk.

And do you know what?

'I'll do it!' he said, proudly, and Buster smiled at him.

Venk had been waiting for a moment like this. A moment in which everyone turned to him. The only problem was, if everyone had turned to him, maybe that meant it wasn't such a great thing to volunteer for.

Obviously, one of Clover's plans would mean dressing up somehow, and Venk wasn't really one for dressing up. But no matter! The team had looked to him and he had risen to the challenge. How bad could it be?

Suddenly there was a **THUMP-THUMP-THUMP** on the garage door.

It was Horatia Snipe, dressed very smartly indeed.

'You look nice,' said Alice.

'Well, I thought I'd better make an effort,' said Horatia. 'Seeing as I'm hosting the Beautiful Baby Competition.'

'You're *hosting* it?' said Alice, who still didn't quite trust Horatia. 'Why didn't you mention that yesterday?!'

'I did tell you I was going to be there, I just didn't go into detail . . .' Horatia said, sheepishly. 'The *Starfish* is sponsoring it so of course that means that, well—'

Alice rolled her eyes. 'Let me guess. A *Frinkley* baby will win?' she said.

Horatia nodded, sadly.

'I'm supposed to give all the awards to Frinkley babies. Apart from **STINKER OF THE YEAR**, which I'm free to give to any baby from Starkley. I've been told to go on the radio in a few minutes and say it's been a cracking year for beauties in Frinkley, but that

Starkley babies all look like fat, bald hamsters.'

'Wait,' said Elliot. 'The radio? Do the radios work again?'

'Yes,' said Horatia, before adding, slightly proudly: 'I'm going on GBC4. *National* radio.'

Hamish began to feel uneasy. If the radio signal was suddenly back, it had to be for a reason.

An annoyed Clover had had enough and stamped her foot in frustration.

'You know what, Horatia?' she said. 'You're supposed to be on our side now. You shouldn't host the competition. You should call it off. You are single-handedly helping to put the *whole world* in danger!'

'That's a very serious allegation!' said Horatia.

'I'm a very serious alligator!' said Clover.

'Why not do something heroic?' said Alice. 'And say, "Forget it! I'm not hosting this blimmin' baby competition! It's cancelled!" I mean, it's *simple!*'

'Yeah!' said Clover. 'It's not rocket salad!'

Horatia looked awkward. She could do that but she'd lose her job. She wouldn't be able to feed her family.

Hamish shook his head.

'They'd just find someone else,' he said. 'And we don't know how Scarmarsh would react.'

He stood up, tapping his chin.

'Plus, do you know what? This is good. We have someone on the inside. In fact, this might be just what we need!'

Finally, and just in time, Hamish had started to come up with a plan.

26

Bawlers

At 9 a.m. exactly, the people of Starkley and the people of Frinkley took their very separate seats.

They were very separate because a) they couldn't exactly all sit on the same seat, and b) they wanted to be as far away from each other as possible. It was Starkley on one side, Frinkley on the other, and, in the middle, a lost tourist called Martin who had no idea what was going on.

'Why does it smell of cinnamon?' he kept asking.

What should have been a lovely competition had started to feel like something less pleasant.

Beneath the balloons and bunting, there wasn't the normal polite chit-chat and hellos that grown-ups always use when mingling with strangers. There were none of those questions they all ask each other when they don't know what else to say. Those questions that aren't really questions, just weird sentences they swap with each other.

Like, normally, one of them would say, 'This weather!'

And then the other one would look around and then laugh loads, like pointing out that there was some weather was really funny.

'Hahahaha, I know,' they'd reply. 'Oh, dear.'

That's not a conversation, is it?

And it was even less friendly now. People eyed each other and muttered suspiciously. They were too busy muttering and sputtering to take a good look at what was around them.

But Alice did. She looked out at the dozens of babies and shook her head. It was worse than she could ever have imagined.

Boffo Quip was surrounded by fearsome infant associates of all shapes and sizes.

It looked less like a beautiful baby competition and more like the Starkley International Champion Junior Weightlifters' Convention. A rather scared-looking lady was selling baked goods next to the face-painting stall, as babies queued up to buy and scoff whole cakes.

'Okay, let's have our first, um, baby!' said Horatia into her microphone, and up stepped Mr and Mrs Popperby. Well, I say 'stepped'. It was more like 'staggered'. They really were struggling to hold their baby between them. Both parents were pretending this was absolutely fine and their baby weighed the same as fairy wings, dreams and rainbows. In reality, he was the size and shape of a sack of potatoes.

'This is Delbert,' gasped Mr Popperby, his legs wobbling at the knees from the strain of carrying his enormous six-month-old baby. 'He has a very special skill.'

'Yes,' said Mrs Popperby, with a sweaty, bright red face from all the effort of their short walk. 'He can crush a can of pop in one hand!'

Right on cue, Delbert whipped a can of Epic Soda from his nappy, opened it with the mere flick of a finger, drained the whole thing, belched and crushed the can in one fat fist. Then he threw it the length of the square and it rattled into a bin.

It was seriously impressive.

'Very good!' said Horatia, as the Popperby parents collapsed under the weight of their can-crushing Buddha. 'Our next baby is from Starkley.'

A couple of Frinkley people nudged each other and smiled, ready to make fun of it.

The Drongs of Starkley both had very long hair and wore

heavy-metal T-shirts. Their little girl was called Marmalade, and apparently she could strum a simple chord on the guitar while her parents sang in close harmony. Mr and Mrs Drong cleared their throats, ready for their performance, but, when Marmalade picked up the guitar, she just started wildly smashing it into the stage!

SMASH!

CRASH!

BASH!

SMASH!

'Marmalade!' shouted Mr Drong, appalled. 'I thought we were going to jam!'

The baby girl rocked her head backwards and forwards as she swung the guitar, like a proper grown-up headbanger with her hair flying everywhere. The noise was tremendous. Horatia kept glancing nervously at Boffo, hoping all this was keeping him in a jolly mood and not angering him.

Boffo simply looked on, barely interested. This was good. Nurse Pickernose had said so in her training.

The guitar had splintered into fifty pieces by now and, even though all that was left was the neck, Marmalade still kept whacking it.

All the babies started beating their chests and shouting, **'Ooh! Ooh! Ooh!'** in rising excitement.

But enormous Boffo just looked weary. He had turned a huge bib backwards and it made him look like he was wearing a robe or cape. He had obviously just had a Big Boy Breakfast at Frinkley's Royal Burgers, because he had one of their little paper crowns on too.

He raised his hand and the other babies calmed down.

'He's like the King Baby,' said Alice, peeking out from behind the stage.

'We need to keep our eye on him,' said Hamish. 'Pickernose said we must be ready the second it looks like his mood is changing.'

That was the plan so far. Hamish and the gang would judge when Boffo was about to turn into Bad Boffo and immediately try and calm him down. They had a few ideas up their sleeves. Hamish checked his pocket for Mum's chocolate Mustn't grumbles. If they could ward off Boffo's bad mood, it might leave them enough time to work out how to stop Scarmarsh's plan.

Hamish studied Boffo very closely, like one of those nature-documentary people on TV studying a pink puma or a cauliflower cuttlefish. Every little Boffo blink. Every twitch of his mouth. Every slaverous globule of baby drool. In one hand, Boffo held a long rattle, like a sceptre. On his chubby knee sat his faithful friend, Toppy Sparkles. But Hamish couldn't see any sign of anything else. No mind-control collar. No tiny radio in his ear. Nothing that gave any hint or clue that Scarmarsh could get to him.

Another baby was on stage now and had somehow set his father's shoe on fire, which made all the babies go crazy again. Frau Fussbundler had to run onto the stage with Madame Cous Cous's beloved red fire extinguisher. Hamish

noticed the babies kept glancing at Boffo, as if desperate for his approval.

But still Boffo stared with little emotion, giving nothing away, like a bored Emperor watching terrible gladiators.

And then . . .

'Did you see that?' said Hamish.

A slight judder of Boffo's knee.

Just a little bounce, nothing that anybody would notice.

And then another.

'Yes!' said Alice, but Hamish already knew something was about to happen, because the radio crew from GBC4 were signalling to Horatia Snipe.

'Thirty seconds, Ms Snipe!'

They were preparing to broadcast right across the country.

'Wait! *That's* why the radio signal is back! It's a way for Scarmarsh to spread the Baby Boom!' cried Hamish, putting it all together. 'He's listening to the radio, and he's going to trigger Boffo the second they start their show!'

Hamish and Alice looked at each other in horror. They'd thought the **BABY BOOM** could work its way slowly round the world. But, if it was *broadcast*, any baby near a radio could hear it and be affected!

Babies in cars.

Babies in shops.

Babies in kitchens or garages.

Babies in barbers.

Babies *everywhere*.

Things were rapidly reaching crisis point.

'How is Scarmarsh controlling him?' asked Alice, as Boffo suddenly threw his rattle to one side and started to grimace.

'I don't know but he's getting upset!' said Hamish. 'Look at his bottom lip!'

It was quivering . . . and shaking . . . and *v–v*-vibrating . . .

Boffo's eyes started to well up with fat, fat tears, ready to spill . . .

He stood and raised his arms, taking one enormous deep breath and lifting his teddy bear – his pride and joy – high into the air.

Its eyes caught the glint of the sun, and in that split second everything became clear to Hamish.

'It's TOPPY SPARKLES!' he yelled. **'TOPPY SPARKLES IS THE KEY!'**

27

Uh-oh, It's Babygeddon!

Buster was on it like a bonnet!

Like a *baby* bonnet!

He'd been sitting in the ice-cream van, engine running, staring at Hamish and Boffo from the other side of the square. The second he saw Hamish begin to panic and wave his arms about, he'd shouted, **'We're ON!'** and jammed his foot down on the accelerator.

The van's huge wheels had begun to spin and squeal as the **PDF** lurched into action, with Clover, Elliot and Venk flying to the back as it shot forward.

Boffo Quip was microseconds away from the mother of all tantrums. His huge eyes were wet with tears that were ready to spill. His chest heaved up and down, gulping in air that in moments he would force out again in some mighty, crazed baby yell. He squeezed both eyes shut, ready to unleash his monstrous powers, thanks to the evil teddy bear that was somehow controlling his mood.

'**It's babygeddon!**' said Venk, pressed up against the window of the van.

'Not if I can help it,' said Buster, skidding into the square and honking his horn to distract Boffo.

Distraction is key, that's what Pickernose had told them.

Boffo, red-faced and with a look of thunder, blinked one eye open. Who dared disturb the mighty baby?

'*Now, Elliot!*' yelled Buster, and Elliot slid back the roof of the van.

Buster hit **PLAY** on his stereo, as Elliot hoisted up the van's huge disco ball. He'd rigged up all manner of torches to shine on it and suddenly 'Twinkle, Twinkle, Little Star' blasted from the speakers!

The babies looked up as the pretty shapes danced around on the buildings, reflected from the disco ball like a night light or a mobile.

240

Some babies, who had been ready for a fight moments earlier, began to sink back into their chairs, or sat heavily back down on their parents' laps (which their parents did not enjoy at all).

'Oooh,' said one baby, as Buster started Stage Two: Feeding.

'Ice pops,' said Buster, flinging them from the van, **'99s, Lemonade Lick-me-ups, Slush Guppies.'**

Babies began to crawl gently towards the van, picking up whatever they could and licking at the ice creams.

Boffo, still surrounded by four or five fierce-looking babies, looked suspicious.

'Stage Three!' shouted Buster.

Clover kicked open the back doors of the van. She'd been hard at work all night. She was dressed in a costume she'd made which she called the 'Baby Calmer'. She had two handfuls of pink glitter, a unicorn's horn and a dress that looked like a puffy cloud. She began to leap and jump around the square, trying to be graceful and throwing glitter wherever she could.

'I'm a cloud!' she yelled. 'I'm a unicorn!'

'*Oooh!*' oohed the babies.

'Babies!' yelled Horatia through the microphone. 'You are

feeling sleepy! It's beddy-byes time!'

Babies that had been moving swiftly began to slow down, fascinated by Clover, calmed by the lullaby, almost hypnotised by Horatia.

'It's working,' said Alice, punching Hamish quite hard on the arm to celebrate.

But Clover kept looking behind her. Where was Venk? She needed backup. He'd seemed fine with the plan. Delighted to be part of it, even. But now he'd lost his bottle.

Clover did some more jumping and sprinkled more glitter. The babies, already relaxed by the very loud lullaby, loved watching it catch the sunlight as it spread in the air and fell to earth.

'Venk,' she half whispered. 'Now!'

But Venk remained in the van, head down.

'*Venk!*' she hissed again, much more sternly this time. 'If I run out of glitter, they'll *get bored*!'

She threw a little more and stared at the van in disbelief. Where was he?

'I have to say, this is the strangest half-time show I've ever seen,' said the reporter from GBC4 Radio, whose listeners must have been wondering what on earth they had tuned into.

One of the babies started to sigh. Clover was almost out of glitter and was becoming much less interesting.

'VENK!' yelled Buster. **'We NEED you!'**

Venk heard these words and raised his head.

'What if this is it?' Buster said. 'What if this is **YOUR MOMENT?'**

And at that Venk found his strength.

He slid the side door of the van open and revealed himself for the first time.

He was wearing the biggest, most detailed, multicoloured Toppy Sparkles costume you've ever seen.

His face poked out of a big Toppy Sparkles head, complete with mad googly eyes.

He had giant paws and a big rainbow tummy.

'I said make me *cool*,' he said to Clover. 'This is the most humiliating day of my life!'

The babies began to shake excitedly. *It was Toppy Sparkles!* Toppy Sparkles was really here!

And Venk decided to just go for it.

'I AM TOPPY SPARKLES!' he yelled, waving at his baby fans. **'I'M TOPPY BLINKIN' SPARKLES!'**

Hamish and Alice had to stifle their laughter. Clover's plan was genius. Hamish knew if there was one thing Boffo loved, it was that deranged bear, and Venk was doing a *great* job.

But their laughter wouldn't last long. Because, while almost every other baby in Starkley began shouting with glee and happiness and joy, and all thoughts of a **BABY BOOM** were starting to fade, one baby did not look happy.

AT. ALL.

'Alice,' said Hamish, batting her arm. 'Look.'

Boffo had turned bright red. His hands were shaking. His lip was quivering. He bent down and clutched his own Toppy Sparkles.

When he'd dropped it, he'd broken the bear slightly. And, on its arm, Hamish could just about make out a couple of wires . . .

'There's something in Boffo's Toppy Sparkles!' said Hamish. 'That's how Scarmarsh must be controlling Boffo – through some kind of mind-control device. Like those teddies that play mood music or whale song. Toppy could control Boffo's mood. And the Formula One made that mood bigger and badder!'

Boffo stared at his damaged Toppy and then at Venk. He seemed to seethe.

'I think he's jealous,' said Hamish. **'He's jealous of the massive Toppy Sparkles!'**

Why would Boffo want his small, broken Toppy Sparkles when a huge, massive, boy-sized Toppy Sparkles was right there waiting for him?

Remember what Madame Cous Cous said? A baby's emotions are pure. Imagine feeling nothing but jealousy.

Pure jealousy. Coursing through your veins. Combining with rage. And being big enough to do something about it.

'It's happening,' said Hamish, as it seemed the buildings themselves started to rumble and quake. 'Somehow Scarmarsh has triggered Boffo!'

Hamish spotted the GBC4 reporter on the stage, with his microphone held up in the air, capturing everything that was going on. 'Alice – you have to stop that broadcast!' Hamish said. 'We can't let other babies hear Boffo go crazy!'

'I'm on it!' said Alice, bursting into action with the speed of a tiger, making a dash for the stage and leaping through the air.

Hamish turned back to Boffo as a single tear dropped from his big blue eyes . . .

Hamish watched it almost as if it was falling in slow motion . . .

Falling . . .

Falling . . .

The purest of baby tears falling.

And – *poff!* – it landed in the scattered glitter by Mrs Quip's handbag.

For a second, it seemed like there was nothing but silence.

28

Cry Babies

'AAAAAARGH!' yelled Grenville Bile, panicking in a way that really should be illegal. 'Gerrem off me!'

As he spun round and around, three little babies hung from Grenville's back, clutching him with one little fist and bopping him with the other.

When Boffo's tear had hit the pavement, the King Baby had immediately **WAAAAAILED** to the heavens, causing a chaotic shift in the other babies' moods.

Hamish had been proud to see Alice diving to knock the microphone out of the radio reporter's hands and then pulling whatever wires out of whatever equipment she could find.

Phew! The Baby Boom was contained! But this was still an earth-shattering, mind-scattering, ear-clattering . . .

Parents tipped over tables and screamed as babies pelted them with whatever they could find from bins and bags. Big brothers and sisters screeched and legged it, pursued by small teams of baby assailants. Two babies picked up a skipping rope and turned it into a tripwire, sending Mr Ramsface and the strange little man from the newsagent's tumbling head first onto the grass.

Two babies clambered through the roof of the ice-cream van and while one of them pulled Buster out of the front door, the other slapped his stereo until the gentle lullaby stopped and insanely loud **HEAVY METAL** came on instead!

Little Marmalade Drong absolutely lost her mind with joy!

The grown-ups didn't know what to do. It was loud. It was mayhem. They were supposed to be in charge. Some of them tried telling the babies off. They stood there, waggling their fingers and making stern faces, not realising there were babies creeping up on them from behind, ready to pull down their pants and replace them with nappies!

One baby pushed a junior trampoline into the middle of the square, and five or six others began bouncing high up into the air to the rhythm of the heavy-metal music before launching themselves at the screaming adults!

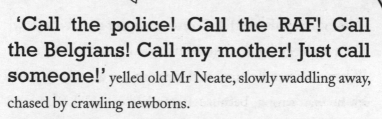

'Call the police! Call the RAF! Call the Belgians! Call my mother! Just call someone!' yelled old Mr Neate, slowly waddling away, chased by crawling newborns.

Call Belasko, thought Hamish. *But Dad's still miles away and this is my mess to clear up!*

He had to come up with a new plan and fast.

'**ROOOOOOOAR!**' came a voice to his right.

It was Boffo! He was towering over the other babies, like some massive sumo wrestler, and he knew exactly where he was going.

He was headed straight for . . .

'**VENK!**' yelled Alice. '**Watch out!**'

Venk had been batting away babies left, right and centre. They kept trying to hug his legs, because of his ridiculous bear costume.

'**TOH-PEEEEE**,' Boffo said in his deep, deep voice, grabbing Venk's arms in his enormous fists.

'**NO, NO!**' said Venk, realising in horror what was happening. 'I'm Venkatesh!'

'**TOH-PEEEEE!**' repeated Boffo, pulling Venk close to his chest.

How was it possible that Boffo was bigger than Venk now?

'What's he going to do to him?' asked Alice.

'I hope just cuddle him,' said Hamish, but already he could see he was wrong, because Boffo had grabbed Venk and thrown him over his shoulder. Now he was bounding over to the town clock.

'Boffo!' yelled Hamish. **'NO!'**

But Boffo had his prize, and wanted to show the world that the big Toppy Sparkles was his! He started to clamber up the clock tower with one arm wrapped round his life-sized Toppy, as smaller babies punched the air and whooped.

Soon he was at the top, towering over everybody, roaring!

'Well, at least it can't get any worse,' said Alice, putting her hands on her hips.

But you know what? It can *always* get worse.

As Venk flailed around in his arms, Boffo looked proudly out over the square, then put two chubby fingers in his gummy mouth and let rip with a piercing . . .

PHEEEEEEEEEEEEEP!

Hamish covered his ears and frowned. Babies don't whistle! That was Point No. 2 in his baby project!

A split second later, other babies began joining in, with whistles so high-pitched and grating that windows started to rattle in their frames and old Mr Neate's dentures fell out.

'What's happening?' said Alice, covering her ears as the **PHEEEEEEEEEEEEP!** came to an end.

And then – distant barks.

Alice stared at Hamish.

The barking was getting closer.

And . . . were those meows now too?

Hamish and Alice braced themselves, as the pitter-patter of approaching feet turned to the thunderous sound of a drum. The last of the grown-ups fled, as from over fences and down drains and across roofs ran dozens of furry beasts.

'ATTACK KITTENS!' yelled Alice. **'And puppies!'**

Of course! Cats and dogs were supposed to be able to pick up on human emotions too, weren't they? And, when an emotion is expressed as powerfully as Boffo was expressing his, obviously it was too much for any animal to ignore!

Hamish looked around, completely startled. It was **dizzying, dazzling chaos.** It was overwhelming. Where was he even supposed to start?! Scarmarsh had somehow created an army out of the things people loved the most! All of them linked by Boffo, like some kind of master computer!

Kittens were now hanging by their claws from Grenville's bottom as he ran for the hills. Puppies were pushing over all the radio equipment. Babies were jumping up and down on Elliot. One infant had pulled Clover's unicorn horn right down over her eyes. They'd locked Buster out of his own van and two of them were peeing on his dashboard. And now Venk was being held hostage up a clock tower by a giant baby who seemed more than mildly in love with him!

Hamish's head was spinning with the scenes around him, but the worst thing was that all of this wasn't even their biggest problem. They might have postponed the Baby Boom from spreading too far for the moment, but Scarmarsh was still out in the woods, with enough Formula

One to infect the entire country anyway.

'What do we do?' Alice asked Hamish in a shaky voice.
'What do we do??'

'DON'T PANIC!' came a voice.

The kids spun round. It was Nurse Pickernose!

She stamped on the end of her medical skateboard and it
flipped up into her hand. She was flanked on either side by
two other mobile nurses called Hilda and Ludwig.

'You've done a good job,' said Pickernose. 'But you made me realise you were right, Hamish. Babies require specialists. We've got this!' She was ready for battle, with bottles of milk in holsters on her hips and refills strapped across her chest.

Hamish smiled. He'd been hoping she'd show up. He knew kebabs were her new love. But he also suspected she'd never be able to turn her back on the babies.

'**HILDA!**' Pickernose yelled, testing the temperature of the milk on her wrist and spinning the bottle back into its holster. 'You take the newborns. **BOTTLETOP BAXTER, YOU STOP THAT RIGHT NOW!** Ludwig – grab the pets. **ORANGINA – PUT THAT OLD MAN DOWN!** I'm gonna tackle the big boy ... **C'MERE, BOFFO!**'

And, as Hilda started scooping up newborns and Ludwig wrestled with attack kittens, Nurse Pickernose unfurled a mega-super-pack of moist towelettes, then ran for the clock tower and began bouncing up the sides like a determined and furious cat.

'We'll deal with this!' shouted Clover, who was wearing a baby almost like a backpack. 'Go get Scarmarsh!'

Hamish and Alice nodded at each other. They needed to get to the woods.

It was time.

29

Alice Turned Around

Down the country lane Hamish sped, his Howler roaring at full pelt, with Alice charging alongside on Blue Streak.

They were a fearsome duo, and both Vespas were packed with awesome new features, courtesy of Buster.

Like Alice's **ElectroGlide** lights, which meant that now everywhere she rode she left a brief, bright blue streak behind her, matching the one in her hair.

Or like Hamish's small plastic sandwich box.

On reflection, Alice's moped was probably cooler.

Alice had insisted they take the back routes out of Starkley so they wouldn't be spotted on any baby monitors. That was super smart. Scarmarsh had to have been listening to the radio broadcast to make sure his Baby Boom had spread. Which meant he would already know the **PDF** had scuppered things.

Hamish was worried about that, because Scarmarsh was so unpredictable. If he felt threatened, he might lash out, like a wounded animal. He was not a patient man and seemed to have this vendetta against Starkley in particular, but why?

His deal with the Superiors meant he could go anywhere in his part of the universe. Why keep coming back to Earth – and why to a town where he knew there'd be resistance?

Alice's eyes were watering: the smell of cinnamon was hot in the air.

Hamish signalled to her to pull off the road, and together they rode along the bumpy dirt track to the edge of the woods.

Each reached over to the back of their bikes and pulled out a sleek new **PPP – Panic Protection Pack!** – and strapped it on. Inside was water, whistles, super-spicy Tabasco sauce spray, Chomps for energy, an old nut and pickle baguette, hygiene gel, walkie-talkies, flares, masks, warpaint, a packet of sweets and a chess set. They'd had time to change into their black **Belasko** boiler suits and now looked ready for anything.

'We don't know what's waiting for us,' said Alice. 'Scarmarsh might be panicking. Or he could already be long gone. Though from the stink of that Formula One I'd be surprised.'

Hamish agreed. Scarmarsh was still around, he was sure of it. They needed to be on their guard, and as they crept through the bracken in the woods, keeping low and moving quickly, they made sure not to step on any sticks or give away their position.

The smell of cinnamon was overpowering now, and Hamish could hear engines.

Peeking through the trees, they saw a flabulous, globulous Terrible with a clipboard barking orders. Its bug eyes were yellowed and its nails scraped at the dirt underfoot. Mushrooms on the ground stretched and strained to get near it, the way flowers reach for the sun. This thing was like a fungus magnet. As he passed trees, giving out more orders, the moss seemed to blacken. The Terribles in the lorries were nodding at everything he said, and pressing buttons inside. The Terrible in the mechanic's outfit they'd seen the last time they were here was tinkering with an engine, getting it to pump Formula One faster and faster with his bright red box of tools.

Hamish hated these good-for-nothing monsters. They were like Scarmarsh's private military. Their stink mixed with the cinnamon from the Formula One and the petrol from the tanks and created a sick-making brew. The kind that made your nostrils flare, and made every sniff feel like someone had jammed two spiky straws up your nose.

Each lorry juddered and thuddered as their tanks pumped

more and more Formula One.

'So they've not gone,' said Alice. 'And it doesn't look like they're stopping.'

Hamish shook his head.

'They're making *even more* Formula One,' he said, as a line of white transit vans driven by Terribles started to pull up by the petrol station.

Each had something different written down the side.

STEAKS ARE HIGH
BUTCHER'S
OF PEPPERMILL

JUST FALAFS!
Falafels and Gags for Thrunkley and Beyond!

WISHY-WASHY
LAUNDERETTE
We'll Clean You 'Urp'!

As they trundled to a halt, Terribles rolled out toxic-looking barrels from behind the petrol station and started loading the vans.

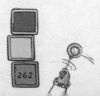

262

'Look – those vans are going to Urp, and Thrunkley, and Peppermill,' said Hamish. 'Alice, I think that Scarmarsh is planning to secretly take Formula One to different towns. Then he'll be able to create loads of new Boffos and start the **BABY BOOM** that way!'

'*Babygeddon*,' said Alice, gravely.

Hamish shot Alice a look that said, *We have to stop this madman from unleashing complete anarchy on the streets of our towns and cities.*

It also said, *We both know our roles here and what we have to do.*

It was a look that *also* said, *Alice, if you're thinking what I'm thinking then grab those tools and set to work immediately while I sneak a closer look at what's happening in the tower, and then wait for my signal.*

'Why are you giving me that weird look?' said Alice, confused. 'Have you got wind?'

So Hamish explained what he'd been thinking out loud, which, on reflection, he probably should have done in the first place.

Alice nodded as he spoke, then did exactly what she'd trained herself to do.

She waited until the Terribles had finished loading their vans.

She SCANNED the 'action area' to work out where her **EXIT POINTS** were in case she needed a swift getaway.

She made a mental note of where the enemy had gone and added it to a **MIND MAP** she was **MEMORISING**.

She **COUNTED** the number of **PACES** it would take her to get where she needed to be, and how **FAST** she'd have to **RUN** to do it well.

She **SCOPED OUT** a number of hiding places – a bush, a tree, a bin – and she did it all in a matter of **MOMENTS**.

And then, her recon of the area complete, she nodded and turned to Hamish once more. Hamish had another very strange look on his face.

Alice slowly turned round and looked up into the warty, bulging eyes of a Terrible.

30

'Whoooooaaaaa!'

Hamish and Alice flew through the air.

They'd been **flung out of the woods** by the ginormous Terrible who was so *very* terrible he could have been called a *Verrible*.

'Whoooooaaaaa!' cried Hamish, wondering if he would ever land.

BOFF!

The kids crashed heavily onto the ground, skidding along in the dirt and coming to a painful stop by the petrol pumps.

When this absolute giant had picked them up by their **PPPS**, he'd held them at arm's length, nipped between his fingers, and grimaced, the way a parent might pick up a sock from your bedroom floor.

He seemed completely and utterly disgusted by this pair of yuklings he'd found in the woods. Yet *he* was the disgusting one!

'He stinks of cinnamon!' said Alice, mentally kicking herself for allowing this awful thing to creep up on her.

'Formula One,' said Hamish, scrabbling to get to his feet. 'Maybe he's been drinking it. Maybe it doesn't just work on babies . . .'

Alice's eyes widened. It was one thing raising a barmy. But Scarmarsh controlled thousands of these Terribles. Maybe millions across the universe. Who knew? If each of them suddenly grew as enormous as this one, there could be trouble!

Well . . . even more trouble than usual.

Now the giant Terrible was coming at them, snarling and snapping off whole branches from trees and casually tossing them aside, as the bushes around them rose and fell with each stomp of an enormous foot.

STOMP! STOMP! STOMP!

The kids looked around, horrified. They had to think quickly. What should they do? Dig a hole? Climb a tree? Make a run for it? But they were surrounded by vans, and barrels, and the Terrible blocked their path to the woods, and how on *earth* would digging a hole help them?

'Hamish, look,' said Alice, pointing at the ground.

A cluster of mushrooms swayed this way and that, as if

attracted by a dozen different things they couldn't decide between. They were like weird little tentacles growing from the ground.

Now the nasty old weeds that had grown round the old petrol pumps were rising and straining too. Black moss started to shake, then fly from the trees, like it was being sucked across the atmosphere. The bad vibes hung heavy in the air.

Hamish suspected this could only mean one thing: a bruise of Terribles was upon them.

That's when it really hit them.

'We're surrounded,' said Hamish, taking off his **PPP** as long, gnarly, angular shadows grew all around him.

A piercing noise shot through the place like an arrow.

SQUEEEEEEEEE!

Alice threw her pack to the ground and poured the contents out. She grabbed a super-spicy Tabasco sauce spray. Hamish picked up a stale nut and pickle baguette and wielded it like a sword, as from all around them fresh, freakish Terribles loomed from behind vans and bushes.

The monsters snortled and sniffed and panted like horses and seemed to grow as they circled the children. Black smoke wisped from warty nostrils.

Which one would move first? wondered Alice, getting ready to fight back.

And, as the first one extended its arms and made a grab for them, Alice sprayed her Tabasco and leapt away. Hamish thwacked it on the back of its head as it spluttered and sneezed and scratched at its eyes.

ROOOOAR!

The Terrible was terribly furious. Its cry was loud and the air that shot from it was like a super-powerful leaf blower. Sticks and leaves and pebbles swirled in a whirlwind around them, making it harder to see. Also, it was pretty clear that the Terrible had eaten fish for lunch.

The kids were back to back now, moving in a slow circle, the full horror of their situation upon them.

Another Terrible lurched itself forward but Alice was too quick.

She spun away again, this time picking up her bottle of hygiene gel and squeezing it hard. A slick of gel shot at the Terrible's germy tummy and began to fizz and spit as it ROARƎD. Hamish delivered another **POW!** with his baguette, but more Terribles were ready to take its place.

'We can't keep doing this,' said Hamish. 'There are too many of them! We need to get out of here!'

Hamish wished he could just whistle and his Howler would turn up, like a magic horse. He really needed to talk to Buster about that – but now was not the time for thinking about magic horses.

BAFF!

Hamish thwacked another Terrible, but the beasts were starting to realise that approaching the kids one by one wasn't going to work.

The giant Terrible raised its hand and held up four disgusting fingers . . .

'What's he doing?' said Hamish, as another ROAR sent more sticks and pebbles flying at them.

Then the grinning Terrible held up *three* fingers . . .

'He's counting down!' said Alice, and she knew exactly why. They were about to pounce!

Alice fell to the ground and grabbed her walkie-talkie as the Terrible now held up only *two* fingers . . .

'PDF! PDF!' said Alice, holding down the red button on her walkie. **'SOS! SOS!'**

ROOOOOARRRR!

A DOZEN HUNKERING TERRIBLES thundered forward, striking all at once and from every angle, grabbing the children from all sides and hoisting them up in the air by their ankles.

Alice watched as her walkie was crushed in a monstrous fist. It sparked and fizzed as a Terrible threw it at a rock.

Had the message got through? Or had Scarmarsh interfered with the radio signal again?

As the kids now bounced around on top of the horrible horde, prodded and poked at, they kicked and sprayed and kept swinging baguettes.

'I need more than a sandwich for this!'

wailed Hamish, still bravely bashing away at the beasts below and flinging nuts and pickles everywhere.

But it was no good. They were outnumbered and outmatched and now they were as good as captured!

'OOH, VISITORS!' came a voice, and the Terribles shrieked in delight. **'BRING THEM TO ME!'**

Hamish and Alice were thrown to the ground once more. As they lay there, Axel Scarmarsh himself stood at the doors to his Post Office Tower, cracked his knuckles one by one and smiled a deeply sickening smile.

31

Things Get Worse

'You truly are pathetic creatures,' said Axel Scarmarsh, walking down the steps to where Hamish and Alice lay on the ground, surrounded by slavering Terribles.

The ground was slick with beastly spittle as it poured from monstrous mouths and noses.

'But catching you is a bonus,' he said, running a hand through his hair and smiling. 'So tell me, where's the rest of your strange little crew?'

'Stopping your mad babies from doing any more damage!' said Alice, always defiant in the face of danger.

'Oh, those babies are just the start of things,' said Scarmarsh, checking the cuffs of his beautifully tailored suit. 'Please forgive my intrusion, young Ellerby. But, when the cat's away, the mouse will play . . . How *is* your father, Hamish?'

HA! HA! HA!

'He's on his way back!' said Hamish, with as much grit as he could muster. 'Him and loads of other **Belasko** agents!'

Hʌ HA! Hʌ

Scarmarsh laughed, arching his long back.

'What a shame he'll be too late. I wonder why he decided to travel so far away? It's almost as if he got some bad information . . . You *do* have to be careful what you read these days. You really can't trust it all.'

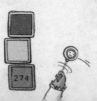

Hamish stood up. It made him feel braver, even though all it did was highlight just how tall Scarmarsh was compared to him.

'Frinkley knows we're not as bad as you put in your paper,' he said. 'Now they've seen us with their own eyes!'

'Ah, yes,' said Scarmarsh, as quite out of the blue a Terrible flicked Hamish's ear. 'How satisfying to use your own things against you. Your suspicion of outsiders. Local papers, people, even babies.'

Up close, as Scarmarsh ran his hand through his hair again, Hamish could make out below his hairline out a small, faded scar, shaped like an X, that he'd never noticed before.

'By weaponising babies,' Scarmarsh continued, 'I could create a fake crime wave to make you turn on each other.'

'The baby burglars!' said Alice. 'In and out through a cat flap!'

'And much more importantly,' said Scarmarsh, 'I could strike right at the heart of what you all hold most dear.'

'And what's that, Scarmarsh?' demanded Hamish.

'Why, *family*, of course,' he said, with a twisted grin. 'Isn't that all any of us really wants?'

Hamish had started to shake a little. Partly out of fear and partly out of anger. He felt Alice reach for his hand.

'By controlling the world's young,' said Scarmarsh, oblivious to anything but the sound of his own voice, 'I control the weakening grown-ups. Through their babies, I can decide how much they sleep and how clearly they *think*. They will be my slaves, as I raise their babies in the ways of Scarmarsh. And, as tradition dictates, I will begin in Starkley.'

'Tradition!' said Hamish, angrily. 'I don't believe it's just tradition.'

'Oh?' said Scarmarsh, smiling creepily.

'It's more than that. There's something else. You've got it in for my dad.'

'I am in the middle of *trying* to tell you about my evil plan,' said Scarmarsh, flapping his cape, a bit vexed. 'Aren't you interested? It's rude to interrupt people.'

'Hamish is right,' said Alice, as another Terrible flicked Hamish's ear. 'Something about this doesn't add up. We know the Superiors have handed Earth to you, so why not start somewhere easier? Somewhere not linked to **Belasko**? There's something you're not telling us!'

For just a flicker of a moment, Hamish thought he saw a flash of doubt in Scarmarsh's eyes. But was it doubt? Or was it sadness? Either way, it was gone as quickly as it arrived.

'I do what I want,' spat Scarmarsh.

This was weird. He seemed rattled. Almost hurt.

'ARE THE VANS LOADED?' he screamed, and the Terribles all flinched at their master's voice. One of them nearly choked on the remains of Hamish's nut and pickle baguette in shock. 'Then start driving. Every hospital in a three-hundred-mile radius will soon receive their free batch of Formula One. Every pharmacy, every coffee shop, every baby store!'

Hamish watched as a Terrible carried a large sign and packed it into a van. It read:

Scarmarsh Industries is proud to deliver a FREE nourishing sample of Formula One to help the country's babies grow and grow and GROW!

This was horrifying. If they didn't do something quickly, Scarmarsh would start a nationwide **BABY BOOM**, raising his barmy of warrior babies!

'Wait!' said Hamish, trying to come up with anything he could to stall him. 'What makes you think you can control all the babies?'

He had a point. One baby, yes. A handful, maybe. But thousands and thousands of them? Hamish thought if he could sow a seed of doubt in Scarmarsh's mind he could prevent this somehow.

'Babies are difficult!' added Hamish, trying to remember exactly what he'd said in his school report. 'They defy authority! They're like impossible dogs! They're absolute nitwits!'

Scarmarsh looked unimpressed. 'I believe that children are the future, Hamish. *My* future.'

'But think of the *nappies*, Scarmarsh! If all the babies grow as ginormous as big old Boffo, think about how massive their nappies will get! You'll have to have special waste grounds! It'll be pull-ups right up to the sky! It'll be a nightmare for you!'

Scarmarsh just smiled.

'Not my problem,' he said. 'As far as I'm concerned, this rotten place is just a planet full of filled nappies anyway.'

The first of the vans turned its engine on. Another followed straight after.

'So why do you want it?' pleaded Alice. 'If this place is so

unattractive, just let it be and go somewhere else!'

'Pah!' scoffed Scarmarsh.

'Wait!' said Hamish, as more Terribles started their vans. 'There has to be something we can do. Something has hurt you, Axel. That's why you're doing this.'

Scarmarsh frowned. He wasn't used to people calling him by his first name.

'Shut up,' he said, and his reaction told Hamish he was onto something. He knew he'd seen a look of sadness in his eyes a few moments before. A memory.

'Something has hurt you, and you want to get even,' Hamish said. 'That's what all this is about. You're not just randomly picking on our planet or our town or *us*: you want *revenge*.'

There it was again. Just for a second, a flicker of something in Scarmarsh's eyes as he ran another hand through his hair, revealing that small X again. Alice saw it this time. Hamish was getting through to Scarmarsh. She nodded her friend on, urging him to continue.

'If you didn't have something else you wanted – something bigger – why would you settle for Part B of the universe?' Hamish said, his brain working overtime, trying to understand what was behind Scarmarsh's targeting of Earth.

'You chose the "Bobbins" part for a reason! You wouldn't settle otherwise; you're Axel Scarmarsh!'

Scarmarsh cracked his knuckles and looked pensive. It was like he was about to tell Hamish something, *admit* something to him.

But . . .

'**START YOUR ENGINES!**' he roared. The rest of the vans and lorries fired up and thick, putrid diesel fumes filled the air, puffing around the kids in a horrible black fog. 'And THROW THESE NOSY CHILDREN IN THE VAULT!'

Two huge Terribles grabbed Hamish and Alice by the arms.

'**Yuklings,**' one of the monsters seemed to say, savouring the word and licking its lips.

'Hamish, what do we do?' said Alice, trying and failing to get free. 'What do we DO? We can't let that formula leave!'

But there was still hope.

Because if you listened closely – very, very closely – over the racket of the engines and the shouts of the beasts, you could just make out the dim, faint roar of a seventy-mile-an-hour ice-cream van.

32

Pitter-patter,
Skitter-scatter!

The **PDF** had heard the SOS!

'Hamiiiiiiiish!' yelled Venk, from the open sunroof of the ice-cream van. **'Get iiiiin!'**

The van burst through the bracken and bushes of the woods and skidded to a halt as Terribles scattered out of the way.

'No!' shouted Hamish at his friend. 'We can't leave yet! The lorries with the Formula One need to be stopped.'

'Get your PPPs out!' yelled Alice, scrabbling to find her Tabasco spray on the ground and snapping back into her attack pose. 'We need to fight the Terribles! Scarmarsh is in his tower and is sending them all over the country to—'

'Guys, we need to go,' interrupted Venk. 'Right *now!*'

Hamish was taken back by Venk's insistence. He wouldn't

normally interrupt. He was too cool to do that. But at this precise moment he seemed a lot less cool. For a start, his giant Toppy Sparkles head wobbled every time he talked.

'**Look out!**' shouted Elliot from inside the van.

Alice started squirting spicy sauce at an approaching Terrible. It squealed and pawed at its eyes. Others were gaining confidence again and creeping back towards the kids.

'You heard Hamish,' said Alice. 'We're not leaving until we've stopped these vans full of Formula One! All of them!'

Buster leaned out of the window. 'Venk's right,' he said. 'We're about to have company!'

Hamish frowned. And then he heard it.

Like a low, rolling thunder.

The pitter-patter of not-so-tiny feet.

'Babies!' said Hamish, eyes widening.

The thunder was getting louder – fast!

'**Even Pickernose couldn't control them all!**' shouted Clover from the van. 'Boffo's love for Venk was too great. When we heard your SOS, we got straight in the van. I thought we'd outrun them, but then I looked in the mirror and they were after us! Boffo wasn't ready to say goodbye to Venk!'

'It turns out he's extremely jealous,' said Venk, rubbing his arm. 'And he's a *very* powerful cuddler. Let's go!'

Hamish couldn't work out what the bigger threat was.

Was it the Terribles?

Or the babies?

Was it Scarmarsh?

Or the Formula One?

It was all too much. There were too many problems. He didn't know what to do. If only he could think more like Scarmarsh. If only some problems *did* cancel each other out . . .

Wait.

'I've got an idea!' yelled Hamish. **'Get out of the van!'**

Venk looked terrified.

'But then I'll be captured by both the babies *and* the Terribles!' he said. 'I'll be grabbed *and* cuddled!'

'Do it!' said Alice, realising what Hamish was planning. 'All of you – out!'

The doors of the ice-cream van creaked open and the kids joined Hamish and Alice.

'I hope you know what you're doing, H!' said Buster.

Around them, scaly Terribles crept closer and rose up

higher and scarier than ever.

'Brace yourselves!' said Hamish, as in one quick movement dozens of Terribles pounced on them, covering them in great globules of slime and spit and hoisting them up into the air again.

'This seems a rubbish plan so far, Hamish!' said Venk, his big, plastic googly eyes rolling around above his real ones. The Terribles began to carry the **PDF** towards Scarmarsh's tower, where Hamish was sure the vault Scarmarsh had mentioned was, and where their enemy planned to keep them for all time.

'Listen!' said Alice, as the thunder from the woods became almost deafening.

A second later . . .

'ROOOOOAR!'

Boffo Quip burst through the undergrowth, his chest heaving.

Behind him, swinging from branches like monkeys and leaping over bushes – a fearsome barmy appeared at his side!

Some babies carried sticks like spears.

Others wielded rattles.

Some were covered in mud, while many had used the face-painting stall to create wild and imaginative warpaint.

It reminded Hamish of what they'd seen in the Holonow – this was just like the Viking horde!

The Terribles stopped in their tracks and turned, stunned to see this fearsome bunch. The **PDF** bobbled in the air as the monsters stood still, wondering why the babies had turned up.

'**TOH-PEEEE!**' grunted Boffo, pointing his giant, chubby fist at Venk.

'Oh, no,' said Venk, even though he should have been impressed that a newborn had such a grasp on words.

But the Terribles were not going to give up their prize so easily. Scarmarsh wanted these kids in the vault and that's just where they were going.

'**TOH-PEEEEE!**' yelled Boffo again, as more warrior babies showed up to support their leader, slapping their chests and hopping from foot to foot.

A group of Terribles broke away and walked towards Boffo, hoping to scare him off. But Boffo wasn't afraid of a few weird monsters. He was big, bad Boffo Quip and someone had stolen his favourite toy.

'*Boffo, my boy!*' came a voice from a loudspeaker. '*It's me . . .*'

Scarmarsh was not coming out of his tower, but he thought he could calm Boffo. After all, he'd soothed his moods in the past using the Toppy Sparkles, and done so wonderfully. You see, there are some sound frequencies only children can hear. And there are others that only *babies* can hear. Scarmarsh had been using Toppy Sparkles to control Boffo's moods through sounds only he could pick up. Perhaps he might play something soothing to calm him. Or perhaps he'd play the sound of a thousand furious rats squeaking and squealing to get him riled up. But that particular Toppy Sparkles was broken now. Scarmarsh would have to try and calm Boffo another way.

'*Easy, boy,*' said Scarmarsh. '*That's not your toy. That's a stinky child in a pretend suit. I can get you another Toppy Sparkles. I can get you two, or three, or four! The best you've ever seen!*'

But Boffo didn't want another Toppy Sparkles. He wanted this big one. The one he'd fallen in love with. And no grown-up or group of Terribles was going to take it from him.

More Terribles tried to block Boffo's path as suddenly the **PDF** were carried up the steps to the tower – and possibly to their doom.

The tears in Boffo's eyes started to well.

His face began to go bright red.

His lips began to quiver.

'Come on,' whispered Hamish. 'Get angry!'

But Boffo just looked sad. Around him, the other babies started welling up too. One of them sat down and started crying.

So did another.

Soon, they were all in tears.

This was a nightmare! Hamish didn't want the babies sad. He needed them mad! He had to have Boffo's enormous influence.

'Venk,' said Hamish. 'Tell Boffo you love him!'

'Absolutely not,' said Venk.

'Tell him you love him!' said Hamish. 'Please, Venk!'

'It's undignified,' said Venk.

'You're literally dressed as a teddy bear while monsters carry you around in front of sad babies,' said Alice. 'It's hard to get less dignified. Now do as Hamish says! **We NEED you, Venk!**'

Venk nodded. He could do this. He'd already dressed up as Toppy Sparkles today. He'd already felt a proper part of the team. But this was his real chance to save the day. His moment to shine.

'I love you, Boffo,' he said, quietly.

'*Louder!*' said Hamish.

'**I LOVE YOU, BOFFO!**' he shouted, now far more determined. '**I LOVE YOU I LOVE YOU I LOVE**

YOOOOUUU!'

Immediately, Boffo's eyes lit up.

He looked at Venk with incredible tenderness.

And then that love began to change into something else, as the **PDF** reached the top of the stairs.

It turned to rage. **PURE BABY RAGE.**

Who were these monsters to steal the one thing Boffo cared about?

'You did it, Venk!' said Hamish, watching Boffo change. 'I think there's going to be a . . .

BABY! BOOOOOOooooom!'

But now the babies were on the side of the **PDF** and the sheer speed of the infants took the Terribles by surprise.

Within just a second or two, they were everywhere!

Angry, punchy babies.

Viking babies kicking at scabby shins.

Ninja babies pulling at slithery scales.

Wrestler babies launching themselves from the top of the van.

Boffo stood and screamed in anger, like a more frightening Godzilla, sending his troops into battle, then running at the Terribles himself and knocking them over like bowling pins.

The **PDF** fell heavily to the ground as the Terribles began to scarper, abandoning their posts and their vans and their leader.

'**Boffo, NO!**' shouted Scarmarsh from the tower. '*Choose power! Not love!* **CHOOSE POWER!**'

But Boffo didn't care about instructions, and he didn't care about power. Boffo had no master. He was in the middle of the most beautiful baby tantrum the world had ever seen and, as he knocked Terrible after Terrible out of the way, he stomped ever closer to proud Venk.

'H-h-hello, B-Boffo!' said Venk, slightly nervously, hoping the inevitable cuddles weren't quite as bruising as before.

'**TOH-PEE!**' breathed Boffo, scooping Venk up and squeezing him until his eyes were approximately three times bigger than they should have been. '**LOOOOVE.**'

And, in that second, that sheer feeling of warmth and full-heartedness spread like a flash of lightning to every other baby in the woods, like a **BABY BOOM OF LOVE**.

The woods seemed almost to glow pink, as babies began kissing and hugging the Terribles, which frightened and disgusted those monsters all the more.

'**YEEAAAACCCHHH!**' screeched one, backing away from two or three babies who were waddling towards him with their arms outstretched for a cuddle. **'AWWAAAY! AWWAAY!'**

Dozens of Terribles turned and squirmed and did everything they could to avoid the affections of these tiny, pure-hearted infants, and thundered away in absolute and total terror.

Then: **FSHEEEEEEEEWWWWW**.

What was that deafening noise? The clearing began to fill with bright white smoke.

Hamish turned to see the doors of the Post Office Tower start to close.

The boosters at the bottom were firing up and beginning to spark – **CA-CLACK! CA-CLACK!** The woods filled with the familiar acrid smell of Scarmarsh's fuel.

'He's trying to escape!' cried Hamish.

Alice looked up at the tower. There was no way in. And, if they somehow did get in, what if it blasted off anyway? It would take them straight into space. She couldn't go into space today. She was supposed to pick up eggs on her way home.

'The lorries!' said Hamish. Just like Scarmarsh had done to Frinkley, Hamish would *use his own things against him*!

293

He ran for the first Formula One lorry and pulled out the giant pipe at the back – the one they'd been using to fill all the petrol tanks and barrels. It was extremely heavy – he needed Alice's help.

She was next to him in an instant, as she always was, helping him lift the pipe as Buster yanked hard at the lever to start the flow.

BOOOOOOOOOFFFFSSHHHHHH!

Out shot the Formula One at a thousand miles an hour, lifting Alice and Hamish in the air for a second as they grasped the pipe . . .

'Aim for the boosters!' yelled Hamish.

Elliot and Clover ran to the second lorry and grabbed its pipe as Buster followed and pulled on that lever too. A great whoosh of Formula One rushed from their pipe, arcing up into the air, chasing the tower as it took off. The powerful stench of cinnamon and diesel pumped out of the lorries as the kids held on with all their might.

Above them, the tower was starting to shudder and judder now.

The **PDF** had the right idea, but were they too late?

Some of the boosters were failing, but still the vast building was rising slowly, slowly into the air. And, the higher it got, the harder it was to hit. They just couldn't lift the pipes any further. This would take serious muscle!

'BOFFO!' yelled Venk, cradled in Boffo's arms as if he was a baby himself. **IF YOU LOVE ME, HELP US!'**

'Yes, Venk!' shouted Hamish.

Boffo flung Venk over his shoulder and stormed over to a lorry, using his giant baby arms to lift the pipe, aiming the Formula One high, high up into the air . . .

And hitting the boosters dead on!

The Post Office Tower was now shaking wildly as it rose above the trees . . . it still had power but not much! It wasn't heading straight for space any more, but towards the sea instead. Scarmarsh was just desperate to get anywhere other than here!

The **PDF** cheered, knowing they had done enough damage: the tower was sputtering and stuttering and belching out huge great globs of black smoke, like full stops across the clear blue sky.

And just as it left their sight . . .

KA-BOOOOOOOOOM!

No. Not the sound of the tower exploding.

But a *sonic* boom, as a fresh trail of fire tore across the sky! Hamish's dad re-entered Earth's atmosphere in his spaceship after racing 163 thousand miles to be there – too late to fight Scarmarsh, but just in time for lunch.

33

Ice Ice Baby

When the ice-cream van rolled back into Starkley, surrounded by a hundred triumphant babies, the cheers and roars of approval were deafening.

Scarmarsh had been beaten. The babies were safe.

Oh, I wish you'd been there. It was quite the sight.

When Hamish's dad had landed in the clearing – and sent his colleagues off to chase Scarmarsh through the air – he hadn't been expecting to see quite so many infants wielding spears. I mean, who ever does? But Angus Ellerby had known precisely what to do next: make sure there was no more Formula One on Earth.

Right now, he and Belasko were taking care of the barrels and 'free samples' Scarmarsh had been preparing.

If there was one thing that was particularly gratifying, thought Hamish, as he clambered out of the van to the sound of cheering, it was that you really couldn't see much of a difference between Frinkley people and Starkley people any more. Everyone looked the same.

They looked happy.

They also looked really, really pleased to see the **PDF**. No more suspicion. No more wariness. Just gratitude.

'Who wants a kebab?' said Nurse Pickernose, running up to the gang, excitedly. 'I thought I'd use up the last of them today and give them all away free!'

'Really?' said Hamish. 'How come?'

'Maybe I was a little quick to give up nursing,' she smiled. 'Today was a wonderful reminder of the old days. And also all my meat's due to go off tonight.'

'How much do you want for it?' asked Madame Cous Cous, who already had plans to release a brand-new Kebab Candy Floss.

The **PDF** smiled as they watched more babies reunite with their parents and the last wafts of cinnamon were carried off on the wind. Everyone seemed to have learned a little something about their families today.

The babies, for example, had learned that home is where the heart is, that power is no match for love and that the

safest place for them was right alongside their mums and dads. And the parents had learned that, deep down, their babies were extremely dangerous trained assassins capable of terrifying and unpredictable acts of violence.

It was all absolutely *lovely*.

'Check out Boffo,' said Alice, nudging Hamish.

The big baby had just sat on a bench and it had immediately collapsed. He still had Venk hoisted round his neck and was sucking his thumb – by which I mean *Venk's* thumb – until he saw Mrs Quip, tossed Venk aside and stomped over to his mother, knocking her clean off her feet.

'I hope the Formula One hasn't affected him permanently,' said Hamish, concerned. 'I mean, the babies will get smaller again, right?'

A moment later, a huge and impressive black motorbike roared into town. An absolute giant of a man in a leather jacket leapt off and ran towards Mrs Quip, tearing off his motorcycle helmet and diving to hug Boffo hard. Hamish recognised the man immediately.

'It's Mr Massive!' he said, delighted. 'Mr Massive is Boffo's dad! No wonder the Formula One had such an effect on him! He was already going to be huge!'

On the stage Horatia Snipe suddenly tapped her microphone.

'Well, if we're all back and ready to proceed,' she said, 'it's time to award the prizes! And I can tell you that for the first time ever ... *all* the babies have been awarded first place!'

Well, this wasn't like Horatia Snipe at all!

Early editions of the 𝔉𝔯𝔦𝔫𝔨𝔩𝔢𝔶 𝔖𝔱𝔞𝔯𝔣𝔦𝔰𝔥 would detail the events of the day in all their glory. The **PDF** would be hailed as great heroes. And the travel section would recommend the wonderful town of Starkley as the region's Greatest Place to Visit!

Plus, as a thank you from the Mayor of Frinkley, not only were the **PDF** given the 'Freedom of Frinkley', but *every* child in Starkley was given free Laser Quest and hot dogs for life.

𝔉𝔯𝔦𝔫𝔨𝔩𝔢𝔶 𝔖𝔱𝔞𝔯𝔣𝔦𝔰𝔥

STARKLEY GREATEST PLACE TO VISIT!

'There's just one thing I don't get,' Hamish said, while the celebrations continued, not even looking up when he felt his dad's comforting hand on his shoulder as the afternoon turned to evening.

'What's that, pal?' said his dad, and the two of them instinctively looked up at the sky, their bellies full of kebab and chips. The moon was out early, and one or two bright stars twinkled in the sky.

And, somewhere out there, was Axel Scarmarsh. Hamish's dad had been just too late. His first instinct had been to check on Hamish. Maybe he was overly protective. But Hamish wouldn't have it any other way.

'Why us?' said Hamish. 'Alice wondered too.'

'What do you mean?' said Dad.

'Scarmarsh has half a universe to play with. So why is he so obsessed with Earth?'

Hamish's dad didn't say anything. He just stared up at those bright stars.

'Like, he keeps choosing Starkley,' continued Hamish. 'He builds a lair not far away. He keeps targeting us. And yet he knows this is the one place where *you* are, and where *I* am. He said it was "tradition", but it's more than that, I know it.'

'I think he'll be back one day,' said Dad. 'Maybe you can ask him.'

'But why?' said Hamish, turning to stare at him. '*Why* will he be back?'

Hamish understood that every hero needs a nemesis. But he'd never signed up to this. He'd never done a single thing to Axel Scarmarsh.

His dad kneeled down so that they were the same height.

'Some people choose love over power,' he said, 'and others choose power over love. I chose love. I think you would too. But Scarmarsh? He chose power.'

'When?' said Hamish, confused.

His dad thought about what to say next. He remembered something from many years before. Something he'd avoided talking to Hamish about so far.

'Remember Mum showed you a photo? The one where I'm fishing?' he said. 'And I'm with my brother? The one Mum told you I fell out with? The one who never spoke to me again?'

'Yes,' said Hamish. 'He fell. He cut his head in that bog.'

'Well, we argued that night, and all the next day. It got out of hand. I'd done something stupid, like kids sometimes do, but the worst thing is I never said sorry properly.'

'I don't understand,' said Hamish.

'My brother fell,' said Dad. 'In the marsh. He got a scar.'

Hamish's eyes began to widen.

'He got a scar . . . in the marsh?' he said, and even as he repeated those words, and rolled them slowly around in his head, he couldn't quite believe what his father was telling him.

So Angus Ellerby made things really very clear indeed.

'Axel Scarmarsh is your uncle,' he said. 'And I have a feeling he wants a family reunion.'

THE END

For now . . .

Frinkley Starfish

Reflecting the best of Frinkley – and our glorious neighbours in Starkley!

INSIDE! Horatia Snipe: *Why I Was Wrong About Everything I Ever Wro*

VENK SAVES THE DAY!

Hero PDF member distracts giant baby!

Could Starkley's famous PDF gang have a brand-new leader? In a startling show of bravery (and fashion style!), it was the wonderful Venk who stood out as the real hero of the hour when noted galactic villain Axel Scarmarsh unleashed his crazed babies on the region recently!

'I don't normally dress up as a giant mad bear,' said Venk, looking awesome and cool and epic even though he was still dressed as a giant mad bear. 'But on this occasion I was in no way against it because I am such a dude.'

The dude, who has always been quite secretive about his talents, then flipped[ ] jellybean in the air[ ] very nearly caught[ ] his mouth, which v[ ] so cool we may ha[ ] fainted.

NEW LOCAL POET LAUREATE

The Starfish is proud to announce that Jimmy Ellerby (twelve) of Lovelock Close, Starkley, has been awarded the title of POET OF THE YEAR after submitting a 10,000-word poem entitled *All the Things I Can See Right Now?*

It begins: 'There's a coat? There's a picture of a boat? There's a cork which can float? This is a poem that I wrote!?'

And goes on for nearly four hours if read out loud.

'I'm extremely happy?' he said. 'Like a really big nappy?

Though I'm fifteen[ ] know why you keep[ ] twelve?'

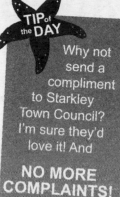

WRESTLING!

MR MASSIVE VS BOFFO

THE BEAST OF BABIES!!!

Frinkley Town Hall, Saturday 2 p.m. Bring a baby.

NURSE PICKERNOS!

returns to Frink... Hospital!

Says on reflection that as a nurse she should not have been recommending kebabs.

MR ELBOWS

Hello, I'm Mr Elbows.

I'm from Frinkley.

We have hotdogs and that's cool.

But Slarkley has Madame Cous Cous!

Hamish Ellerby Would Like to Thank…

… his pals at Simon & Schuster (in particular Jane Griffiths OBE, Elisa Offord MBE, Jack Noel POP and Laura Hough OMG). Also due thanks are Robert Kirby and Jane Willis. Jane Tait too. Seems like more Janes than usual. And final thanks to EB, Clo and Kit for all the ideas you give Hamish and his pals every single day.